THE ASSASSIN'S HEART

ALEXIS ABBOTT

Get an EXCLUSIVE book, **FREE** just as a thank you for signing up for my newsletter! Plus you'll never miss a new release, cover reveal, or promotion!

http://alexisabbott.com/newsletter

CHARITY

$\mathcal{I}$f there's anything my parents have instilled in me over the many years of homeschooling I have received, it's that people cannot be trusted.

No one is good.

Especially men.

So as I search desperately for the locket I lost under the hotel bed, and I hear the telltale sound of heavy footsteps, my heart begins to race.

I can't be found here.

Maids in this hotel have been fired for much less.

I can hear faint, deep voices in a quiet, serious conversation, and then the click of a card key sliding through the sensor. My stomach turns. These guys do not sound particularly friendly at all.

Just as the doorknob is turning, my fingers close around my locket. But I don't have time to get out of here, and I can't be caught snooping around the floor of these strangers' hotel room.

I decide that my best choice is to stand up and face the door, ready to smile sheepishly and apologize for being in their room past check-in hours. But when I try to bounce back up, I realize with a yelp of pain that one of the loose locks of my hair has somehow gotten tangled up in one of the coils under the bed! I'm stuck!

I do the only thing my body is programmed to do: I flatten myself to the ground and shimmy underneath the bed completely, clutching the locket and praying like crazy that these guys don't notice me hiding here.

I am *so* going to get fired. It was a panic response and I instantly recognize how dumb it is, but it's too late.

I hear the door click open and from my position under the bed, I can see two sets of men's boots walk into the room, shutting the door behind them. One of them wanders into the bathroom while the other stands in the doorway looking at him.

I start to sheepishly shuffle to the edge of the bed, to take my chances with an apology, say I was still cleaning up their room and got delayed. But then I freeze when I hear what they're saying, my blood running cold.

"We're talking murder here. Are you sure you're up for this, kid? This is serious. I'm not talkin' about child's play here, you understand? The blood's gonna be on *your* hands, nobody else's."

I clasp my hands around my mouth to keep any sound from escaping.

This can't be happening. No, this can't be happening. Not to me. Not here. Not now. I've always been the good girl. Sheltered. Careful.

Becoming a maid at a middle-of-the-road hotel is not the ultimate dream job I had in mind when I graduated with a bachelor's degree in biology two months ago. I poured so much energy, so much blood, sweat, and tears in the hopes of later going on to veterinary school.

It can't end here, underneath a cheap bed in a middle-of-nowhere hotel, caught by two guests as they discussed... What, exactly?

Blood on his hands.

Murder?

They can't mean that literally.

I do my best to push the thought out of my head. They must be actors. Maybe they're just rehearsing some lines back and forth, trying to remember them. I once found a fashion magazine on the bus—they were strictly forbidden in our house—and they talked about actors and actresses and how to practice for your roles.

And stuck beneath a hotel bed, my hair being painfully tugged by the coil, my breathing held, my body aching as I desperately try not to move, that sounds a lot more plausible than it being anything dangerous.

Why didn't I just let my parents send me to the nunnery like they wanted? Instead, I secretly applied to university, got as many scholarships as I could, and went off to try to save the world in my own way.

And look where that got me.

My homeschooled life, being totally sheltered from alcohol and boys and fun and adventure, helping to raise my 6 siblings, being preened to be the perfect wife... It was all so safe, so secure, so... boring.

But this isn't the adventure I wanted. My mother always told me that I was too naive to handle the great big world out there, and that sticking close to home, living a simple, modest life would suit me best.

As my heart thuds, and I hear the growled voices

of the men in the room grow darker, I think she and my father were right.

The world is too dangerous for me.

Men are too dangerous for me.

Even a job as a hotel maid is too dangerous for me.

I hold my locket tight, squeezing my eyes shut and trying to drown out the sound of their conversation above me. My grandmother gave me the locket, and I always wear it. When I realized I had lost it in the last room I cleaned, I rushed back to find it. It's a source of strength, and I've always kept it close to my heart since she first gave it to me when I was nine.

She was my confidante, the one woman who believed I was strong and capable of so much more than my parents wanted for me. All of my bravery comes from her, and I hold the locket tightly in my hand, trying to channel that bravery now.

My heart begins to beat more rhythmically, and my brain clears enough to think again.

I'm going to get through this, I promise myself. *I won't even get fired. It's all a misunderstanding. I'm just a maid who dropped her locket and went back to get it. Everyone will probably just think it's funny that some young woman would lose her head if it weren't attached to her neck.*

I start to feel a little bit better, bravery rising in my chest.

And then, in an instant, in a single phrase, it all fades away.

"Do you need a gun or do you already have one?"

I don't trust the look of this guy.

But if I want to bring my plans together, I might just have to take a chance. It will all depend on whether he turns out to be wasting my time with this job. It wouldn't be the first, and it wouldn't be the last.

The man looks to be in his late twenties, about my age. That's unusual for my clients, but not unheard of. Chances may well be that he's a middleman for some rich old fucker higher up the food chain.

That, or he might be the solo act he presents himself as.

He has been sketchy with the details, which gives me a bad feeling in my gut, but in this line of work, that game of trusting and second-guessing your instincts never ends. The man's eyes are as black as his hair, and he has the same rugged look about him that I do. If I didn't know better, I might suspect that this is another man in my line of work trying to outsource a dangerous job.

When you deal in blood, anything is possible.

I'm cautious. I am always cautious, but the stakes of this job are high enough that I can cut no corners, and my client is of the same mind. Half an hour ago, we met up in the hotel lobby, pretending to be friends from high school catching up. I walked up to this man who I'd never seen before and embraced him with a smile as fake as his, and I had to hold myself back from cringing at the smell of his cheap cologne. It made him smell like the inside of a locker room in a middle-class suburban community center.

We chatted for a few minutes over a drink at the bar, even though it was only around 2:30 in the afternoon. But at a hotel like this one in the middle of King of Prussia, Pennsylvania, where businesspeople were coming and going faster than anyone could keep track of, nobody cared. Anonymity was one of the perks of working in a big city like Philly. Even with our cover stories, we were practically invisible.

I greeted him by the name Gabe, as he had instructed me before we met in person. I didn't believe for a second that Gabe Hutz was the man's real name. At least, I hoped it wasn't, because if it was, this guy was such an amateur that I'd need to pull out while I still could. But he handled himself like a professional all the way through. Over a drink, he chatted idly, pretending to catch up on how the past few years have been. He pretended that he was passing through for his cousin's wedding, and I pretended I was a local who stuck around Philly and put down roots. To the outside observer listening in, we looked perfectly normal, down to the moment that he invited me up to his room to see a wedding present his uncle was giving him.

Minutes later, here we are.

His demeanor changed as soon as the door closed behind us. He was more nervous than he let on, and that almost made me feel more at ease. It was more like what I was used to.

I've spent years building my career. I started with the lowest of the low, killing men who were already wanted criminals or presumed dead, the types of scum that would never be missed. I made the right friends and dealt with the right enemies, and over time, I built trust. Clients came back once they got a taste of how efficient I could be.

Half the time, I even scare myself with this skill I never knew I had.

But this has been my life ever since my first kill. Ever since I ran from home. It's the only life I have, but I've made something out of it. Maybe it will be something I am proud of one day. But I don't pretend it's anything other than what it is: blood money.

I am a hitman.

There is no way around that.

I didn't ask for this life, but I found myself nudged into it inch by inch. Maybe it's the fact that I'm an adrenaline junkie at heart. Maybe I was just in the wrong place at the right time. Or maybe I'm truly the black-hearted killer that haunts my own nightmares.

Right now, I'm just a man discussing a job.

"Are you sure you're up for this, kid?" Gabe asks behind my back. I make my way into the room, looking around. I first step into the bathroom, flicking the lights on and peering inside. I move to the shower curtain and pull it back, then turn around only after making sure nobody is there.

In the mirror, I see my reflection looking back at me. I'm a few inches taller than my client, with short brown hair and pale green eyes. I haven't shaved in a few days, and the scruff is growing as rugged and wild as it always does.

"This is serious. I'm not talkin' about child's play here, you understand? The blood's gonna be on *your* hands, nobody else's," Gabe continues, watching me from the entrance of the bathroom. I turn my eyes to him, a steely gaze meeting his. He shouldn't be saying anything until I'm sure the room is clear, much less talking about murder.

I move past him without a word, pulling open the closet and checking inside briefly before moving to the main area of the room. My eyes rove over each facet of the place—from the drawers under the television to the desk by the window to the nightstand to the large bed, freshly covered in sheets.

I step over to the curtains and slowly draw them closed, panning over the parking lot below to make sure nobody is watching from downstairs.

I take a few steps toward the bed, peering down at it thoughtfully, eyes roving over the covers, then down to the space below the bed frame.

"You listening to me?" Gabe says suddenly, sounding a little irritated by my silence.

"Yes," I say simply, my gaze meeting his once more, my sweep of the room complete.

"Look," he says as he approaches the desk and sets his briefcase on it. "I know all of this is...a lot, but I don't want this fucked up."

Let him get pissed off. If he doesn't want to be careful and keep us from getting arrested, that's his problem, and I won't let it become mine. I've never fucked up a job and I'm not about to start now.

It makes me worry that this man is not quite as

experienced as the amount of money for this job he's promising suggests. But it's too early to tell just yet, and so far, he has made good on all his promises, despite his jumpiness. Even if I still have the slime from our first handshake on my palms, his money is as green as anyone else's.

"Do you need a clean gun?" he asks, his hands on the briefcase as he looks over his shoulder at me. "I've got a .22 here that can get the job done just fine."

"I use my own," I say in a low but firm tone. He gives me a look, but he doesn't argue with the even gaze I'm giving him. I wouldn't trust any gun Gabe wants to give me. This man is slimy, but he looks like no killer I've ever met. I would be surprised if he even knows what 'clean' means in this line of work, and for all I know, it could be some shoddy piece of shit that will be more of a liability than anything else.

Contract killing was not the first thing I turned to when I started down this dark road, but I found that I liked it partly because I have complete control over every aspect of it from start to finish. Barring whatever special conditions the client specifies, I decide when to strike, how to strike, how to make my approach and escape, and what weapons to use. Gabe isn't the first man to think he can hand me a gun and hope it impresses me.

Gabe and I lock eyes for a few moments, but he nods at last.

"I just want to be beyond sure that all our bases are covered, understand?" he says, stroking his chin anxiously. "This isn't your everyday job."

I nod slowly. He was like this when we were only talking online, too, constantly nagging and beating around the bush. It was like a fly buzzing around my head, and it was growing more annoying by the moment. But I need the money bad enough that I'm willing to put up with him a little while longer.

"It's got to make a splash, you understand?" he says, pacing back and forth a little. He keeps looking from the briefcase to me uneasily. "It has to make the entire city stand up and take notice."

I nod again, and I get the sense that my silence is frustrating him almost more than his overbearing cologne is annoying me. That makes me want to say even less. Maybe I'm just a contrarian at heart. But the more time I spend around this man makes me like him less, despite the money he's offering. And the fact that he wants this to 'make a splash' tells me there's a much bigger ego at work just under the surface. This is a man who wants to know he's responsible for something big. Despite what he says, there will be blood on his hands as well, and he knows it.

There is a kind of voyeuristic kick men like him get from pulling the strings that take lives. If his targets weren't some of the worst people imaginable, I would keep from indulging this disgusting fantasy of his. But if this man is worse than the men he's paying me to kill, I will be impressed.

"There's going to be a lot of heat," he says, looking at me meaningfully. "Can you handle that?"

I let the faintest smile cross my lips before I nod.

He picks up the briefcase and sets it down on the bed, sliding it over to me. "Good. Here are the details. I hope it goes without saying that this information puts a big, red target on you, so deal with it when the job is done."

I don't react to his statement as I take the briefcase and pull it toward me, making note of the security code he has on the lock before clicking it open and looking at the contents.

There are papers within containing so many details about the targets that they themselves would probably be shocked to read them all. My eyes scan over every details.

Two men are detailed in this job. The first of them is named Desmond Lamar, a wealthy man in his late forties who lives in an upscale neighborhood I recognize. The client has provided me with details of his schedule, as he likes to spend time at home. That will be the site of his execution. He is a married man with two kids, both of whom have basketball practice on weekday afternoons, leaving the house almost empty. His wife Janice is a stay-at-home mother, and she poses the biggest risk for the hit. But Desmond is a man jealous of his privacy and 'personal time', meaning he is often away from his wife even in his own house.

I am to leave the body on site after the deed is done and be gone like a shadow. I glance over the details Gabe has produced for me on him. I see an internet search history that paints a very ugly picture of the seemingly quaint father of two. His tastes in pornography would raise an FBI agent's eyebrow, and he spends so much time chatting with sex workers online that some cam girl probably has a fat bank account with him to thank for it. His wife doesn't know about any of this, but she will probably find out after I'm done with him.

That might make things easier on her, actually. There are pictures of him begrudgingly entering a marriage counseling office with his wife, and I somehow suspect it hasn't been very effective.

I look down at the details of the second man, Gerald Callahan. His profile is so similar to the first man's that they might as well be the same person, except that Gerald is more of a socialite than the other. He also happens to be in the running for political office, hosting a party for the Fourth of July weekend. The day itself was yesterday, but tomorrow is when his party is planned. One man dies tonight, the next tomorrow.

I'm scanning Gerald's details when I see Gabe pull out a burner phone from his pocket. "The first half of the money is in your account now," he says. "Do you want to check it on your end?"

I take out my phone and scroll through a few pages until I see what I need, and I nod.

"Five hundred grand now, the other five hundred grand after it's done. I'll know," he adds.

One million dollars is the price tag on these men's lives. It's almost hard to believe. But this is the kind of job I can't pass up.

It isn't just my career on the line, here. There's so much more at stake that Gabe doesn't need to know and never will.

"Do you need anything else from me?" he asks, glancing at the door. "I'd rather get out of here sooner rather than later. Do you think it'll look suspicious if I leave before you?"

"I won't be far behind," I say.

"Good," he says, wringing his hands. "Good. I uh, I'm gonna take a leak while you look that over." He starts to make his way to the bathroom door as I peruse the files, but he pauses. My muscles start to tense. I know there's still a chance this is a trap of some kind, or worse, a sting operation. I'm armed, and I can act fast if I need to. Gabe turns his head just enough to speak to me, and I'm poised to hear him try to put me under arrest.

"If you can pull this off, there could be a real future for you, kid," he says.

And with that, he pulls the bathroom door open and leaves me alone for a few moments. I take a deep breath once he's gone, feeling relieved. I work best alone, not with some mouth breather looking over my shoulder.

I stand up and make my way slowly toward the window with the pictures of the men in my hands. I memorize every detail of their faces, committing them to my mind. I imagine all angles I might see them at, and I picture what might change with a haircut or a shave.

While I stare at the photos, I realize the lighting is getting darker. Clouds are passing over the sun outside, dimming the lights in the hotel room.

At least the weather matches my mood.

But as I turn around and see the room in new lighting, my whole body freezes.

My eyes are on the space under the bed. When sunlight lit the room through the thin curtains, there were dark shadows under the bed and nothing more. But now that the room is darker, I can clearly see something under the bed.

It's a knee, just barely in sight, its owner trying to make themselves as small as possible near the center of the bed.

My heart races, and a thousand possibilities flit through my head.

Maybe this is a sting. It could be an arresting officer waiting to trap me as soon as I try to leave the room. My hand twitches, wanting to go to my gun. But I know if it *is* a cop, it's already over. I'd be better off not putting up a fight. But I don't know that it's a cop at all. It could be anyone, truthfully.

I carefully move back to the briefcase and put the papers inside it, shutting it and locking it tight before I hear the toilet flushing and the sound of the bathroom door unlocking.

There's only one way to find out the truth.

CHARITY

I've never been so terrified in my whole life.

Not even the time I accidentally got separated from my mom at the farmer's market when I was seven.

Not even when I secretly checked out that horror novel from the library and read it in bed and gave myself nightmares when I was twelve.

I wish I could go back to those more wholesome concerns. I'd rather *anything* besides hiding under a bed, too frightened to move or even breathe too deeply for fear of being discovered by a potential *murderer*. I fight the urge to pinch myself, wondering if maybe this is just some bizarre, hyper-realistic nightmare I'm having. But no. I can tell by the way my chest aches from holding my breath and from the musty scent of the mattress I'm hiding under that this is incredibly, totally, painfully real.

How did this happen? It feels like I must have fallen out of the boring story of my life thus far into a scary story some kids might tell around a campfire in the woods. My lungs are burning. I am desperate for a deep breath. I know it's a huge risk—if these guys hear me breathing they will find me.

What will they do to me if they find me?

Hurt me?

Maybe even kill me?

But I know for a fact that I can't hold my breath much longer. My eyes are watering, tears streaming down my face as I plead with God to save me.

Finally, I can't hold it in any longer. I open my mouth to suck in a long, slow breath, trying to stay as quiet as possible. Thankfully, just as I take a deep breath, there's the sound of the toilet flushing from inside the bathroom, which helps mask the sound of my inhale. A rush of relief passes over me as my lungs expand with air at last.

My vision clears enough to realize that in my breathlessness, my leg had twitched forward slightly, and I quickly pull my limbs back towards myself once more, shrinking as much as I can and praying that little screw up won't cost me my life.

One of the men is at the window, his shoes pointed towards me.

Did he see? He doesn't bend down to look under the bed, but my knee was so far out...

How did I end up in this topsy-turvy world where even taking a breath is dangerous? Where having my leg just slightly out of bounds could mean my life? What did I do to deserve this?

I know what my parents' answer would be: that I earned this unpleasant fate by racking up some serious sins. First of all, I betrayed my mother and father's trust by applying to and attending college behind their backs and against their wishes. Second of all, I'm keeping another big secret from them right now: that I'm planning to save up, move out, and go to vet school.

Suddenly, I feel guilt trickling in alongside my fear. Did I really bring this down upon myself by being a bad daughter?

I shake the thought out of my head. My more pressing question is how do I get out of this room alive? I need to get past that first step before I can go back to my boring, quiet, modest life and try to right my wrongs.

Alright, alright, I get it, I think to myself bitterly, *I've learned my lesson. Honor thy father and thy mother or there will be terrifying consequences. Point made.*

If I end up dying in this crappy hotel while wearing a hideous maid's uniform, I am definitely going to haunt the place. My heart starts pounding as I slowly, cautiously turn my head a fraction of an inch so I can flick my glance out into the room.

A jolt of fear passes through my body. I notice that one of the men is still standing there, his toes pointing toward me.

Did he see me? There's no way he didn't see me. In fact, he's probably just biding his time, waiting for the best moment to attack me. He could be toying with me, like a game of cat and mouse. He's the one with the claws. I'm the squeaky, helpless mouse trembling under the bed.

I stifle a gasp as the bathroom door clicks open and the second, heavier man comes trudging out. I hear him zip up his pants and I can't help but wrinkle my nose in disgust. The man heaves a sigh.

"This is an important mission," he says quietly. "I trust that you understand the gravity of the situation, yes?"

"Of course," murmurs the first man, the one who is next to the bed.

I can sense the tension between the two of them, and I get the feeling they don't particularly like each other or know one another very well. Like perhaps they are meeting for the first time. But why now, then? And why here? Am I really just so unlucky that the *one* time I accidentally misplace my beloved locket, I fall directly into a den of vipers?

"You're a man of few words, eh?" the heavier man goads, trying to get a rise out of the first man. My eyes widen and the breath catches in my throat again as I listen.

"My mother has a saying, 'The less you speak, the more you hear.' I try to live by that quote. Hasn't steered me wrong yet," comes the smooth reply. I find myself a little intrigued now. What kind of mercenary murderer guy loves his mom enough to quote her like that?

"Your mama sounds like a smart lady. What do you think she'd say if she knew what kind of risky business you're gettin' yourself into?" chides the other man. My heart beats faster. Both men are speaking with relatively calm tones, but I can tell the tension is ramping up. They clearly do not like each other.

There's a painfully long pause before the first man answers somberly, "You're right. My mother is a smart woman. Smart enough to know when to stay out of my business. You could take a leaf from her book."

I grimace, feeling my stomach twisting into knots. Is this about to be a fight? Right here? In the hotel room? Perhaps that might be a good thing. If they start fighting with each other then maybe I could finally get a chance to make a break for it. Except that my stupid hair is still tangled in the coil. I roll my eyes up to look at it, swearing internally. The men continue talking, so I gradually move my arm up, careful not to make any noise, to pull my hair free of the loop.

"No need for hostility, friend. We're on the same side here, are we not?" says the heavier man, clearly backtracking. They may hate each other, and he may be the one with the money, but I can tell that he's afraid of the first man. Which does not bode well for me.

The first man starts moving and I freeze up, terrified that he might move closer to the bed and kneel down to look at me or something. But to my mild relief, he walks around to the other side of the hotel room, closer to the other man. As if he hasn't seen me. As if he doesn't know I'm still hiding under the bed.

Is he toying with me, or is there some small miraculous chance that he truly didn't notice me?

"I'm on nobody's side," growls the first man. "That's why I work alone."

"Sure, sure. Got it. Secrecy and all that. You're a lone wolf."

"If that's what you want to call me, then sure."

"Truth be told, man, I would rather not call you anything at all. I don't want anybody to know I know you, understand? I hired you so I could keep my hands clean. So the less I know about you, the better."

"Good. We're on the same page."

The heavier man chuckles grimly. "Right. Well, for a five-hundred-thousand-dollar contract, I should sincerely hope so."

"You mean a million," corrects the first man bluntly. The heavier guy groans, and I can just feel him rolling his eyes.

"Right, right. Yeah. Of course. Semantics," comes the flippant reply.

The first man takes an aggressive step closer and the heavier guy stumbles back a little, leaning against the bed and making the mattress sink down slightly, pushing the springs down further on me.

I have to bite my lip to keep from gasping in surprise. I close my eyes tightly and hold my breath again. While the men are talking, an idea occurs to me. I instinctively reach down to my pockets, searching for my cell phone, thinking maybe I can type out a quick SOS text to one of my coworkers or, hell, even my mother. But my fingers fumble around uselessly, my heart sinking as I remember that I don't have my phone on me. Of course. My manager confiscates our phones and makes us keep them in a locker during our shifts.

I really am alone in this situation. Just two guys talking casually about murder, and me—a sheltered, terrified girl with no self-defense training whatsoever.

"Let's get one thing clear from the jump: this paycheck isn't just semantics to me," hisses the aggressor, and I can just tell he's leaning in, glaring into the other guy's face. I feel sick to my stomach. This dude definitely isn't playing around. If he's willing to intimidate the guy who's paying him, then I can only imagine what fate he has in store for me if and when he catches me under here. I don't represent a paycheck. I just represent a nuisance, and I assume he'll deal with me the same way one might deal with an infestation of raccoons in an attic. I send a silent wish to the heavens, asking for protection, although I have a sinking feeling that nobody can help me here. I'm well and truly on my own.

Meanwhile, the heavier man is trying to scoff and play off the intimidating like it doesn't bother him one bit, but his tone betrays the true fear in his voice. "Lighten up, will you? Sheesh. A million dollars. Whatever!" he says hastily.

"Do you want me to lighten up or do you want

me to kill a man? Can't do both," says the first man, as if it's the most casual statement in the world. His cadence tells me it's meant to be kind of a joke, but neither of them are laughing.

"Alright, you can stop bustin' my balls. I get it. I'll leave you to it, alright? Just—don't forget who you're answering to," surrenders the second man. I let out my held breath as he stands up straight again, the mattress bouncing back up.

"I know what I'm doing."

"Right. I'm out then. Good luck," says the second man. I can see his feet carrying him over to the door. It swings open with a creak of the hinges.

As the second man lingers in the doorway, the first man says solemnly, "I don't need luck." And with that, the heavier guy leaves. The door clicks closed and now it's just the mercenary and me. I was hoping he'd leave as well, that I'd get some break, some chance to run.

Are they looking for me yet? I left my cleaning cart outside the last room I was cleaning, further down the hall. But they'd never assume I was in a guest's room, especially not an occupied one. And I know for a fact almost all the cameras in the hotel are for show. The others are just live feeds of the bar area and lobby. Not even a recording to review.

I swallow the lump in my throat as my heart

starts to race. I just know that at any second now, that man is going to kneel down and grab me out from under the bed. But to my surprise, he merely walks into the bathroom, flipping on the light. He closes the door, but not all the way.

Still, I realize, this might be my best and only shot at escaping.

I take a deep breath and summon every ounce of strength and courage in my body, then quickly shimmy out from underneath the bed, still clutching my locket in my hand. I clumsily get to my hands and knees and start crawling toward the door, my heart pounding so painfully in my chest that it's difficult to even breathe properly. I'm only a few feet away—I'm so close to freedom, to yanking open the door, hopping to my feet, and making a break for the elevator. I can get to the hallway and start screaming for help. I can grab hold of whoever comes walking by, hide behind a guest or a busboy or something, anything to put some distance between my body and the killer in the bathroom.

But my bid for freedom is cut short just as I reach up for the shiny golden doorknob. Two large hands grab hold of my shoulders and yank me back, hooking under my arms to pull me up to my feet and drag me backwards.

I open my mouth to scream, but a hand hastily

shoves between my lips. I instinctively bite down, but the hand doesn't budge. This guy has a pretty damn high tolerance for pain, totally unruffled by my weak attempt to fight back.

He is way, way stronger than I am. I realize with a jolt that not only is he much taller and broader than I expected, he's also startlingly, bizarrely good-looking. All this time I've been picturing some brutish, middle-aged caveman. But instead, the face of the man looking down at me with fierce green eyes looks more like that of a menswear model in a magazine. Sharp cheekbones, strong jaw, sleek nose, intense dark eyebrows, and again, those bright green eyes.

I'm so startled by his looks that I forget to fight back as he shoves me down onto the bed. I scoot back against the pillows, pulling my knees to my chest and making myself as small as possible. He rounds on me, looming over the bed and glaring down at me. He's not in a rush. His movements are measured, controlled, like a jaguar stalking his prey.

This is it, I think to myself, *this is the last thing I'm going to see before I die.*

But although his hands are curled into tight fists, he doesn't take a swing at me. He doesn't lunge for my neck or pull out a baseball bat or anything like the bad guys in movies. In fact, nothing about him looks villainous at all. If not for the angry look on his face, he would actually look like one of those hand-some actors on billboards around town. He looks... like some kind of dark and dangerous Prince Charming.

"You and I need to have a little talk," he says softly. "But you have to promise not to scream. Got it?"

I can only tremble and nod, too terrified and in shock to respond just yet.

He comes around to the side of the bed, sitting on the edge and leaning over me to brace both hands against the headboard. His face is only a few inches from mine. I can scarcely remember to breathe as those green eyes pierce into my very soul. I get the sense that this man will know if I lie to him. He can tell.

"What is your name?" he asks calmly.

"Ch-Charity," I choke out breathlessly. He nods.

"That is a lovely name. Okay, Charity. I'm sure you had a very good reason for being under this bed, and from the looks of you I assume you weren't there intentionally to eavesdrop on my conversation with my business partner. That's some seriously rotten luck on your part," he says. "You heard everything, didn't you?"

I open my mouth with the intention of cooking up a lie, but I can't. I've never been a good liar, and right now, all I can think about is being as obedient and timid as possible. I need to survive this encounter, and I know there's no point in fighting. He can overtake me without even trying.

"I-I'm just a maid," I whisper. "I wasn't trying to eavesdrop."

"I'm sure that's true," he agrees. "Unfortunately, you still managed to overhear some very sensitive conversation. And that makes you a bit of a problem for me, you see."

I whimper, already bracing for him to hurt me.

"Please don't kill me," I breathe, tears burning in my eyes.

He frowns. "I don't kill women," he says flatly.

I take very little comfort in his statement. I doubt I can trust him to tell me the truth.

"Ah, Charity," he sighs, shaking his head. "What am I going to do with you?"

"Let me go? I-I won't tell anyone what I heard. I s-swear," I mumble.

He gives me an almost pitying smile. "I wish that was good enough. But you're a part of this now, whether you like it or not." He pushes back and contemplates something for a moment, then stands up and shrugs off his leather jacket, tossing it at me. I let out a little yelp of fear, which turns into a full-on gasp when I see him pull a tiny gun out of his back pocket and point it at me. My heart skips a beat and I brace for the inevitable. His eyes are cold, but his words are soft when he speaks to me.

"Put on the jacket," he instructs. I hesitate, confused by the request. But when he lifts an eyebrow expectantly, I rush to obey. With shaking hands, I pull on the jacket, which is way too big for me.

"Good. Now stand up," he adds, still pointing the gun at me. I acquiesce, though my legs are so weak I can barely stand on my own. I whimper as he walks over to me and slowly, carefully slides the gun up the back of the jacket. I can feel the cold, round mouth of the gun pressed against my back, and I know somehow, instinctively, that he's aiming for my heart from behind. The man gives me another deceptively kind smile and begins to lead me toward the door.

"Where are you taking me?" I murmur.

"You and I are going to take a little trip," he answers cryptically, opening the door and nudging me out into the hallway. "And act natural. We're just a happy couple walking around together. Smile, Charity, and remember that if you scream or disobey me in any way, I'll put a bullet in your heart."

I can feel her strained breathing under my jacket through the metal barrel of the gun I have pressed up against her back. Her heart is pounding a mile a minute even though she managed to keep her cool all the way down the hall. She isn't bad at this, I have to admit. But I'm nowhere near foolish enough to mistake her skill for trust.

This situation is still much more dangerous than I planned for, and we're a long way from the finish line.

She takes a deep breath as we watch the elevator doors close in front of us, giving us a look at our own blurred reflections in the shining metal. The elevator starts to take us down, and we stand in uncomfortable silence for a few seconds.

"There's a camera on us," I murmur. "Act like what we look like—a young couple that just got finished having some fun in a private room."

After a moment's hesitation, she turns and looks up at me wearing a fake smile that could have fooled me, if I didn't know better. She bumps her hip against me, and I smile back down at her, returning the gesture playfully.

"The cameras saw us come in separately," I say with a flirty smile on my face for the cameras. To the silent recording, it will look like I'm just talking dirty to her. "If anyone asks, we know each other from high school. I accidentally walked in on you while you were cleaning. We took a little time to catch up. I insisted on you wearing the coat, because you looked cold."

"What a gentleman," she says. My smile grows ever so slightly more genuine, but I shift the gun against her back to remind her that I have her on a short leash for the time being.

"You're doing great," I say.

"Most of the cameras aren't real anyways," she admits, and there's no lie in her tone. I raise my brow, but don't say anything about her giving up that information willingly.

"Sure you haven't been held hostage before?"

"Beginner's luck," she says tightly, regret in her sweet voice.

"Play your cards right, and I'll let me use you as a reference for next time," I say as our elevator reaches the ground floor, and she stiffens up as she prepares to make her way through public with me again.

"Wait, what time is it?" she asks suddenly as we slowly step out of the elevator.

"Almost four," I say in my normal tone. She bites her lip as we walk toward the hotel exit, and I flit my gaze down to her as much as I can without looking too conspicuous. "Why?"

"I...I need to sign out from work," she whispers. "It's the end of my shift. It'll look weird if I don't sign out on time."

My heart pounds almost as hard as hers is. I can't look at her well enough to tell if she's lying, and if she is, it sounds like a damn good lie.

Can I trust her?

No, of course I can't, but whether she's telling the truth in this particular case could make or break this escape. We don't have time to deliberate. I have to make a call on whether or not to trust her just long enough to sign out from work and come back to me. There are so many things wrong with it, so many risks I'd be opening myself to. But if she's telling the truth, then walking out the door with her without telling anyone and without clocking out will look even more suspicious. I don't even know if she has friends among her coworkers.

I'm flying blind with nothing to rely on but my instincts.

"Fine," I say at last. "Lead the way."

I feel her heart flutter rapidly at my words. She must be as surprised to hear them as I was to speak them, but I can see the logic in her words, even if they're misleading.

She takes a turn to the right, and we start making our way toward the hotel offices, presumably where the employees go to get changed and handle signing in and out each shift. As we walk, I make a mental note of where we are in relation to the outside. I cased this place before entering, like I do to almost any building I set foot in for anything related to work. If I'm keeping track of our direction right, there isn't a building exit from the offices. I saw maids coming and going from the front entrance on my way in, and the other entrances they use are ones open to other guests, not any that looked like they were employees-only on this side of the building.

"You won't be able to follow me in here," she whispers.

"Do you expect me to just let you go?" I growl lowly.

"I swear I won't run," she says, and I can hear the edge of fear creeping through her voice. "I'll just sign out, get my stuff, and come back to you. There's no way out through here anyway."

"Do you know what's going to happen if you start talking to people while you're in there?" I say, the threat clear in each syllable of my voice. She swallows hard, and she nods her pretty head. "Two minutes," I say. Before she can move, I reach up and grab the scruff of the coat's collar, just in case she planned to lurch away from me and expose the gun. I slowly slide the jacket off her shoulders and let it drape over my forearm, which I bring to my abdomen as I fold my arms and lean back against the wall. I nod to her.

She lingers just long enough for our eyes to meet, and for once, I see in her a person who's almost completely unreadable. After that, she hurries through the door to the back room, and she leaves me alone.

Fear is a powerful force, but I don't know if it will be powerful enough to keep this young woman under my control for the next few minutes. As I wait, I find my gaze drifting around the lobby, and I start to wonder if I'm not already compromised.

A receptionist glances my way now and then, and my heart races. Has she found a way to get word out? She might well have talked to somebody as soon as she was out of my sight. That would be foolish. A man with a gun like me is liable to do just about anything, and the time between now and when the police arrive could mean life or death for a lot of innocents, if I were a lesser man who didn't have such a grip on his nerves.

I realize I'm starting to feel paranoid. Even the other hotel guests are starting to look suspicious to me. Granted, I'm a man well over six feet with broad shoulders and a leather jacket draped over my arm. I can blend in, but I can't help if I draw glances.

I shift uncomfortably, feeling my skin crawling. This is a complication I did not need. I sensed that meeting with Gabe was going to give me trouble, but I didn't think it was going to be this tense. How many seconds have passed? Have they turned to minutes yet? I gave her just two minutes explicitly to be unrealistic and scare her into hurrying, making her think I'm a potentially loose cannon. Am I being taken for a fool this very second?

Just as these thoughts run through my head, a voice to my left gets my attention.

"Excuse me, sir-"

I jerk my attention to the voice, and my hand

grips the pistol, ready for anything, expecting to see a police officer standing in front of me.

Instead, the teenage bellhop before me flinches at my sudden movement, and he gives me a nervous smile as he clears his throat.

"Sorry, didn't mean to sneak up on you!"

"It's fine," I grunt.

"I-I just wanted to ask if you were checking in, or if you had any bags I could help you with," he says.

"I was just leaving, actually," I say. "Waiting on someone."

"Oh, I gotcha," he says, straightening up and looking a little more confident that he recovered the situation. "Anything I can help carry out to your car, then?"

"No." My face has an expression on it that clearly says I don't want to be bothered, but teenagers have never been known for being good at picking up on social cues.

"Great," he says. "I hope you found everything to your liking during your stay. Was everything up to your expectations?"

This guy's really fishing for a tip.

"Yes."

"Wonderful!" he says. "Can I get you anything while you wait? Coffee? Tea?"

I have half a mind to just shoot the kid and be

done with it, but instead, I reach into my pocket and pull out a rolled-up $5 I got in change for gas on the way over here. I hand it to him with a half-smile, giving him a curt nod.

"I'm good, kid. That older woman at the door looks like she needs your help more than me." He blinks and he looks surprised at the sight of a woman who couldn't have been younger than seventy hauling two large suitcases through the hotel's sliding doors.

"Right," he says, running a hand through his hair and hurrying away. "Thank you sir, and have a nice day!"

I let out a deep breath as he trots off, but as soon as he's gone, I sense another set of eyes on me. I turn to see the girl standing there in front of the door, staring at me with a surprised expression in her honey brown eyes.

My eyes flit to a clock on the wall, and I smirk at her.

"Good timing."

She gives me a tight smile, and I can almost hear her voice retorting "You didn't give me a choice" in those expressive eyes of hers. I look her up and down. She has changed out of her maid uniform in stunning time. The new outfit is much more flattering, I have to admit, but also remarkably modest. She wears a plain white t-shirt under a green cardigan, and her khaki skirt falls safely below her knees. The locket around her neck is a nice touch to the conservative ensemble. She's not the kind of girl I expected to be taking hostage, but I'm even more surprised that I like what I see.

"Got everything?" I ask, quickly moving to her side again and making sure the gun is pressed against her back through my jacket, even though we look a little more conspicuous than I'd like.

"Yep," she says in a tone that's a combination of sweet and nervous. With any luck, any eavesdroppers will think that she's just my blushing date, and I'm the rugged boyfriend her parents don't approve of leading her out from work. All of that hinges on whether or not she actually kept her mouth shut.

"Then let's go." I prod her with the gun, and she sets off with me, heading toward the doors, past the bellhop and the old woman. I can feel the tension in her. It would be the easiest thing in the world for her to shout for help before we step out of these sliding glass doors, and everything would be over for both of us.

Logic doesn't always come into play in situations like this.

Before we know it, we're out in the parking lot.

"Where are you parked?" she asks. I gesture in the direction of my motorcycle at the far end of the lot, and she swallows as I lead her that way.

My bike is one of the few things in life I can truly call my own, and I love it. It's simple, elegant, jet-black, and it's in top condition, thanks to my hobby of getting my hands stained with oil working on it late into the night. It's one of the few places I can find peace, and it feels good to build something every now and then, rather than destroy.

After what feels like an eternity, we reach my bike and come to a stop. Charity looks down at the bike, then turns her head to look up to me with such a pristine expression of innocent fear that even my cold heart feels wrenched.

"What happens now?" she asks in a thin voice.

That's a hell of a question.

The girl has been remarkably compliant so far. The fact that I haven't heard sirens coming my way or the sounds of boots on the ground rushing toward us tells me she hasn't tried to alert the authorities...directly, at least.

"Give me your phone," I say firmly.

"What?"

"You heard me."

She stares at me for a moment, then slowly reaches into her purse and pulls out her phone, handing it to me.

"Unlock it."

She brushes a lock of soft, brown hair out of her eyes as she nods, and with a shaky hand, she swipes the unlock combination on the touchpad. I make a mental note of it, committing it to memory the first time it crosses my gaze. She hands the phone to me again, and I reach over and take her hand in mine so that I can keep a grip on her while I scroll through her call history.

No calls anytime in the last few hours, and no texts, either.

Either she was smart and quick enough to delete her call history before she left the back room at the hotel, or she truly didn't try to get a call out while she had the chance. Charity doesn't look like she has the guile for that, but I've been surprised in the past, and I won't underestimate anyone anymore. Not even a terrified maid.

I pocket the phone and quickly open the bike's saddle, loading the briefcase into it and shutting it tight, but not before taking out a long, freshly washed rag I usually use for wiping my hands off after tending to the bike. I glance over my shoulder.

Nobody is making their way out of the hotel at the moment, and the parking lot is relatively empty.

"Put this over your eyes," I say, handing her the cloth and letting go of her hand long enough to pick up the helmet off the handlebar.

"What?" she asks, incredulous. "You mean…"

I crack a gruff smile. "I'm taking you somewhere for a surprise, honey. We're a young couple, remember? This is a surprise date, and you can't see where we're going," I add meaningfully. Her jaw sets, and she seems rooted in place for a few moments.

"You're…you're taking me?"

"What did you think I meant by going for a ride?" I say.

She opens her mouth to protest, but her eyes go down to my arm, still covered by a jacket and still holding a pistol that's trained on her. She takes a breath and nods before blindfolding herself.

Once I watch her tie the knot snugly, I quickly slip the helmet over her head, concealing the fact that she's blindfolded. Romantic cover story or no, it isn't a good look to drive down the road on a motorcycle with a blindfolded girl in plain view.

I climb onto the bike, and I help her get seated behind me.

"I've never ridden a motorcycle before," she says nervously. I pause, then take my jacket and slip it over her shoulders again, helping her get her arms into it.

"Keep your arms wrapped around me," I say. "I will drive carefully. Don't get any funny ideas, because jumping might seem like a good idea, but we'll be in traffic, and you won't know what's behind you."

She nods quickly, stiffening.

Once she's on the back of the bike, she puts her arms around me and hugs me tight. She's nervous, and her hands are shaking, but we need to get moving fast.

I turn the engine on, and it roars to life as I back out of the parking spot and start rolling down the asphalt, out the parking lot and onto the open road.

We're out.

But it's far from over.

This girl is going to complicate things, there's no doubt about that. So far, she has proven both obedient and clever enough not to blow my cover, which is more than I was hoping for. I've tried to keep the thoughts away, but as her arms hug me from behind, I can't help but admit that she's more beautiful a hostage than I could have hoped for, too. The way she carries herself makes me wish we'd met under different circumstances. Her large brown eyes are enchanting, and the freckles across her nose are begging to be kissed. But I've only ever seen that face in fear, and unless I want to see that face in a courtroom from the witness stand, that's all I'm ever going to see of it.

The only question now is what to do with her once I'm at my destination.

There are a whole lot of brand new sensations and experiences pinging off of me at the moment, and if the circumstances were just a tad bit less harrowing, I might even be enjoying myself.

I have never known a person who owns a motorcycle before, much less ridden on the back of one. I have grown up in a neighborhood of minivans and sensible four-door sedans. Family vehicles, with stick-family decals and "baby on board" stickers on the rear windshields. Lots of fuzzy steering-wheel covers and brightly-colored kiddie car seats on the inside. And that's just the way my parents like it.

Usually, on the rare occasion that a motorcycle goes barreling down our street in front of our house, my father frowns disapprovingly and makes a snide comment about "disturbing the peace" or "showing off." The last time it happened, there was a huge commotion because the loud rumble of the motorbike engine woke up my baby brother from his nap as it passed by. Cue the screaming and whining from little Caleb, as well as the ranting and raving from my annoyed mother. I had almost nothing but negative connotations for motorcycles and those who rode them.

But this? This was something else entirely. Something totally unexpected. The exhilarating sensation of a massive, hot, vibrating hunk of glossy black metal between my legs. The refreshing, cool wind ruffling through my hair and tickling my bare neck. The roar of the engine, so cocky, so masculine. The scent of my rugged captor's leather jacket, such a manly smell, musky and deep.

I feel a little thrill remembering how oddly considerate it is for him to have given me the jacket, to keep my bare arms from getting cold as we ride along. And there is the unique, titillating sensation of my arms wrapped tightly around a total stranger—a dangerous, handsome stranger at that. I can feel his taut muscles rippling under the thin fabric of his white t-shirt as he flexes his arms on the handlebars and leans around corners. Every time he revs the engine, I can feel the vibration jolt through my body, head to toe.

Well, I certainly never expected my day to go this direction when I trudged into work this morning prepared for a usual boring eight-hour shift of scrubbing toilets and dodging that one busboy who seems to have a crush on me. If not for the electric fear and dread coursing through my entire body at the mystery of what this devilish stranger is planning to do with me, this could be a pretty sweet experience.

If only.

Except it's not just some hot date with a bad boy I'm on right now. I'm not just bucking my parents' rules and regulations to go on a fun joy ride with a hot, off-limits man in a leather jacket.

He has a gun, and not just for show, either. Judging by that conversation he had with the man in the hotel room, this guy means business. He's not afraid to use that gun. If he's perfectly willing to open fire on an unsuspecting stranger for a paycheck, then what is there to stop him from shooting me, too?

After all, I'm nothing to him. I'm no real threat. If I wanted to rebel against him and try to make a move to save my own butt, that opportunity has passed. Sure, while I was in the locker room changing back into my street clothes and retrieving my stuff, I could have made a quick call or text. I could have barricaded myself in that room and called 9-1-1. I could have fashioned a weapon out of one of the spare curtain rods or tools stashed in the corner of the closet there. I could have tried any number of things to protect myself and redirect the trajectory my mystery mercenary has set me on.

But in the end, I decided against it.

Because although I have never been in a situation like this, and nothing even remotely like it, I still have my instincts. In the two minutes allotted for me to get my things, change clothes, and clock out of my shift early, my mind was racing in a million directions. I followed several different paths of logic, and none of them led anywhere good.

If I had called or texted someone for help, who knows how long it might have taken for them to arrive on the scene? And would anyone have taken me seriously anyway? I mean, it's kind of a far-fetched story to explain. 9-1-1 might think I was a prank caller.

My parents would admonish me for making up stories and tell me lying is a sin.

Who else was left? Aubrey? There's nothing she could have done, and besides, she's probably at work right now, not checking her phone.

Besides, now I'm glad my intuition warned me away from using my phone, because as soon as we stepped out of that hotel into the parking lot, Mr. Murderer grabbed it from me to check and make sure I didn't use it. Who knows what would have happened if he had caught me sending a message?

And what would he have done to me if I screamed for help?

If I barricaded myself in the locker room?

If I came out brandishing some useless weapon almost too heavy for me to effectively wield against him?

In the end, he's the one with a gun. I may be sheltered and inexperienced in the ways of the world, but I'm smart enough to know you don't bring a curtain rod to a gun fight. I could have gotten hurt or killed. Or worse, I could have gotten someone else injured or killed. I shudder to myself on the back of the motorbike. I couldn't live with myself if my actions led to the harm of some innocent bellhop or hotel guest.

And I have a strong feeling my captor knows all of this. He knows exactly what he's dealing with and how helpless I am against him. He is the one in control, and all I can do is hold on tight while he drives me to god knows where to do god knows what to me.

I'm just a terrified, overwhelmed young woman with a blindfold on. And that—the fact that I can't see where we're going—is enough to remind me just how much danger I am in. He wants me to be disoriented. He wants me to be lost.

That can't be a good sign.

My parents may have kept me from watching what they call "dirty movies" (which generally refers to any and all cinematography that's not animated and targeted toward children under ten years old), but they couldn't keep me from watching the evening news. I have heard horrible stories about young girls being captured and driven out to the middle of nowhere to be assaulted, murdered, decapitated—the list of terrible things a man can do to a helpless woman seems to be endless.

Clearly, Mr. Murderer is taking me far away from the scene of my kidnapping, and it's important to his plot that I don't know where we're headed.

Still, even though I can't see, I do have my other senses at my disposal. I can't hear much over the roar of the impressive engine, of course, but my sense of smell is still pretty sharp. King of Prussia is a fairly small suburb of Philly, but it's still big enough to have that smoggy city smell, at least to me.

It's a scent of industry, of gasoline and smoke.

It's the only place I have ever lived, and I would like to think I know it pretty well by now, despite the fact that my parents have done their best to keep me locked up safely in the family home.

The suburbs have a familiar, comforting smell and feel to them that I would recognize anywhere. And for a little while, I cling to the faintly flickering hope that maybe we will pass by someone who knows my family. Or maybe a miracle will occur and we will go blazing down the street where I live, and my mother will stomp outside angrily to glare at the loud, disruptive motorbike driver only to see me on the back of it.

Maybe she will recognize me instantly, even in such a bizarre context, with a blindfold over my brown eyes. Maybe she will scream and alert the neighbors. One of them will panic and call the cops. My sister Chelsea might be quick enough to jot down the license plate and description of the motorcycle to include in the missing person's report.

Logically, I know all of this is pretty out there. The chance of someone, anyone, recognizing me and alerting the authorities on my behalf is slim.

Still, a girl can dream, right?

It's not like I have a better plan besides... hope.

But as we ride on, I can feel a change in the air, in the smells and the vibrations around me. I have no idea how long we have been on the road. At first, I did my best to keep track of when we leaned into a left or right turn, making a mental map in my head so that maybe I could retrace our path once we stopped moving and I miraculously broke free of my captor. But by now I have lost track.

Too many turns and swerves. Too many miles packed away as we rumble on down the road toward a mystery location, toward what I imagine will be my final resting place.

After all, that's how these things always end, right? The girl doesn't magically learn how to fight back. She doesn't materialize an effective weapon out of thin air and instantly know how to use it. An angel from the sweet heavens above doesn't descend upon the scene to pick up the helpless damsel and carry her off to safety.

That's what happens in those inspirational films my parents play for the little ones. But in real life, nothing goes so smoothly. I am doing my best to come to terms with what will most likely happen to me: my good-looking, mysterious Prince Charming will morph into a beastly villain and add my name to the long list of people he's eliminated.

And by now, I know we are far from town. King of Prussia is falling away behind us, along with the last shimmering shreds of hope and optimism I have left. Now we are quite literally rumbling off into uncharted territory, at least, uncharted to me.

Because if we are leaving the city smells behind, that must logically indicate that we are heading west. And north. Away from the familiar suburbs of Philadelphia and into the backwoods countryside full of tiny, empty ghost towns and tall trees.

At first, it's just the lack of smog I notice. And then there are new smells. Freshly cut grass, chlorine pools in backyards, and even the occasional whiff of a barbecue pit. Charcoal and spices. Cooking smoke and tender meat. I'm a vegetarian, but the smell still reminds me of simpler times, happy days when my father cooks up a veritable feast on the grill, even taking care to grill mushrooms and peppers for me instead of hotdogs or hamburgers.

The combination of smells around us paints a pleasant domestic portrait of families relaxing by the pool, kids squirting each other with water guns, a mother calling out for everyone to come grab a plate. I could almost muster up a wistful smile if not for the true, gritty reality of what's happening to me.

Because these lovely smells fade away, too, replaced by the less familiar smells of pine trees and firs, muddy trails and, finally, truly fresh air. We are in the country now, well and truly.

How far away do we need to get before we stop? How many miles can the gas tank of the motorbike handle? I don't even know if my captor has a specific destination in mind or if he's improvising. Maybe he's just getting as far out of dodge as possible before finding a secluded area to dump my body.

That thought makes me shiver and my blood runs cold. I wonder what the news articles will say about me. I wonder what kinds of assumptions people will make about my decisions. Will they blame me for my own untimely demise? Will they use me as a learning device for their little ones?

Don't be like Charity Rivers. She was stupid. She was weak. She didn't fight back. They will accuse me of going along with it, of being a willing participant in my own murder. Maybe they'll comfort each other with the thought that I went willingly, that I'm just so dumb that my fate is inevitable, and that no one else could possibly be this idiotic.

Don't worry, I can hear them saying, *that won't happen to us. We're too smart and tough and competent, unlike that silly little girl who never even tried to escape.*

It hurts my heart to think that they might twist the narrative that way, make me a damsel in distress instead of a smart girl in a dire situation.

A scary situation. A murderer with a gun, trained to my back. A two minute window for an impossible escape. A hope that if I just comply, obey, please, that I might make him see me as a person. As someone who isn't a threat.

I can't take him in a fight, but I might be able to convince him to let me live.

Because I know myself. I know I'm not dumb. I'm sheltered, but I'm smarter than people think I am. And most of all, I am cautious.

It's just bad luck that has brought me here.

Right?

But the more I think about it, the more frustrated and confused I get. Maybe those imaginary newscasters are right. Maybe I should be trying harder to fight back and escape. Perhaps I should pull some crazy, dangerous, desperate maneuver in a last ditch attempt to break free.

What should I do, though?

Loosen my death grip on my kidnapper and launch myself off the motorcycle? Roll off the road into a ditch and just pray to god I don't shatter every single one of my bones in the process?

I heard a news story about a woman who jumped out of a vehicle to escape her abusive partner, and she was struck by another motorist right away. As if to tell me to stop thinking about it, I hear the rumble of a transport truck rush past my side and I shiver again.

I'm not going to die here.

Besides, even if I did jump off the bike, he'll be able to catch me in no time. I'm blindfolded, and if I let go for one second to remove it, he will know immediately. The tiny, crucial bit of credit and trust I've built up between us will dissolve in an instant.

The motorcycle careens around a dangerously sharp curve and I let out a whimper of fear, unable to see what's going on, but Mr. Murderer grabs my hands and presses them harder into his chest, keeping me secure while we cut the corner.

It's almost kind of sweet.

Sweet?! I think to myself with a disgusted jolt. *Come on, Charity! You can't think of your captor as sweet. Isn't this a little early in the game for Stockholm Syndrome to kick in?*

Not long after that, the roar of the engine softens a little, and the wind feels less intense. If I didn't know any better, I'd say we're slowing down. And to my surprise, I'm correct. With a few more minutes of the engine sputtering, we roll to a halt and he cuts the engine. The bike leans to one side and he deftly slides off the seat, grabbing me and setting me down as effortlessly as if I weigh nothing at all.

My body feels a weird sort of numb, the vibrations having gone up and down my body so long that the lack of them is... off putting.

"Where are we?" I ask softly.

"Doesn't matter," comes the quiet response. I open my mouth to protest, but promptly close it again, realizing there's no point. If he doesn't want to tell me, I can't make him. Besides, the last thing I need to do right now is further antagonize my captor.

I'm already at his mercy. Why make it any worse?

"Is this where you're going to kill me?" I ask, my voice squeaky with tears and pain, but he doesn't answer. Still blindfolded, he takes me by the hand and leads me away from the motorbike, away from the road.

I can tell by the leaves crunching under my feet, by the weeds and bushes brushing against my legs. I smell pine and mulch, the pleasantly dank scent of moss growing on tree bark and rocks. A few times, I nearly trip and fall over a log, only for my captor to delicately catch me and hold me steady.

Is he trying to keep me safe? Or just trying to keep me from leaving evidence?

He leads me deeper and deeper into the woods, until we are surrounded by the wild chorus of chattering birds and buzzing insects. I wonder where we're headed, and I can't imagine it's any kind of house or structure, not this far into the forest.

Finally, we stop and he grabs me by the shoulders. He pulls off the leather jacket and walks me backward against the thick trunk of a massive tree. He reaches around to drop the jacket down on the mulchy earth, then presses me down to sit on top of it.

"What's going on? What are you doing?" I demand to know, my voice trembling with terror. I shiver and whimper as a rough cord presses against my arms several times. He's tying me to the tree!

"No. No! Please, don't! I-I promise I won't cause you trouble. I won't tell anyone about what I heard in that hotel room, I swear. You can trust me. Promise!" I insist desperately.

"I really wish there was another way to go about this, but I have a job to do, and I can't take you with me," he explains calmly, almost apologetically.

"Oh no. No. You're not going to leave me here, are you? There could be wild animals! What about bears? Or-or wolves?" I splutter, my heart racing.

"I won't be too long. I'm a quick worker," he assures me.

"A quick work—what?" I repeat, trailing off as the realization of his intention crushes me like a steamroller. I can scarcely breathe. "You're not. You won't. You aren't really going to *kill* someone tonight, are you? Th-that's crazy!"

"You already know too much, Charity. It's better if I don't share the details," he replies. Satisfied with the knots he's tied, he stands up and starts walking away.

I cry out after him, "Please don't leave me here! I'm scared! Don't go!"

"No one will hear you out here," he reminds me softly. His tone is more pitying than threatening. "I will return for you. Try to stay calm, Charity."

"Calm? How in the—stop! Come back! Please!" I yelp, straining against the rope. But there's no use. I listen to his footsteps crunching over dead leaves, getting softer and softer as he walks away, leaving me alone and vulnerable, tethered to a tree in the middle of the wilderness.

JAKE

The ride from the waterfall to the little town of Sheffield is one of the hardest I've ever had to make in my life. It isn't for the usual reasons. I'm confident about the job, my bike is in good condition, I'm as well equipped as I could possibly want to be, and time is on my side.

And of course, the pay is spectacular.

But Charity has gotten in my head, against my better judgment.

I can't stop thinking about her. From the moment she was on my bike, something about her felt more *right* than I've felt in a long time, and that bothers me. She's just a hostage, a liability. She's a threat not just to this job, but to my life as a free man.

I still don't know what I'm going to do with her.

The longer she's with me, the more dangerous she

becomes. I've been biding my time, until some miraculous option appears that means I don't have to kill her.

I don't kill women. And I don't kill innocents. I've done horrible things, but my conscience can't handle her death on my shoulders.

And as I blaze down the road, something tells me the longer I spend with her at my side...the harder it's going to be for me to get rid of her, however that is.

I know the safest thing to do that doesn't rob me of my humanity is to come back where I left her tied up after the job is finished, collect her, and leave her blindfolded somewhere. Preferably somewhere remote but close to a place where she can find help and be long gone before she can get a read on where I'm going.

Worst case scenario, she tries to report me, with nothing more to go on than my looks. I know she didn't get a look at the license number on my bike. By then, I'll be long gone.

Best case scenario, she plays it smart and forgets about me while I try to forget about her.

But that face is imprinted on my mind, and I keep thinking back to it. I can still smell her on me, even as the wind whips around my body along the road. I need to clear my head, damn it, but she won't leave my mind.

In another life, maybe.

That is the best comfort I can offer myself. In another life, I'd like to imagine the two of us running into each other at a bar, maybe at work. I could see myself taking her out somewhere for a nice dinner and a little romance, maybe a ride along the coast with nothing but the moonlight lighting the way for us.

I know it's foolish of me to let my imagination run wild like that, but I sometimes find comfort in thinking about the life that I could have had, if fate hadn't intervened. I didn't choose this life. I wouldn't be in it, if there were another way.

But as beautiful as she is, from her rich, dark hair to those large, expressive eyes to that figure that I can't shake from my mind, her appearance isn't the only reason she's in my mind. There was something about that look in her gaze. There was so much fear mixed with defiance, and it looked all too familiar to me.

I know what living with those two emotions is like. I grew up with almost nothing but them, all my young life. They were my comforters and tormentors until I was a teenager. They were my only means of survival. Fear kept me motivated, and defiance kept me pushing. One always spurred the other on in an endless cycle until I left home.

Until I got out of my step-father's shadow.

That is one thought I definitely can't let infest my mind right now. I blaze onward, seeing the scattered lights of the sleepy town of Sheffield in the distance, and I know I'm closing in on my prey. I keep Charity in my mind as I draw near, and the thought of coming back to collect her is the one thing that keeps me focused.

Half an hour later, I'm carefully making my way through underbrush, approaching the house where my target lives. I parked my bike behind an abandoned mechanic shop a few blocks away after slowing down enough that it would be difficult to hear me coming into town. In a small town like this, that kind of caution is necessary. It isn't like Philly. People notice more out here, especially a city-slicker like me blazing in with a motorcycle and a gun.

I creep through the bushes and trees toward the house's backyard, which doesn't have a fence. The lights are on inside, illuminating nearly every room. I case the property carefully, making a detailed mental note of every little thing. Circling around to the front, I see two cars parked—one per parent, I imagine. A basketball hoop hangs over the garage door, telling me the children probably take their hobby outside the practice court. I watch the windows for a long time, trying to get a read on the residents.

The first thing I notice is the lack of children. As expected, they must be at practice. But I only have a half hour or so before they get back, given the time. Taking care of Charity took longer than I expected, and I'll have to be quick.

I see a middle-aged woman appear in the kitchen, looking disheveled. There's a very specific kind of tight frown on her face as she gets out a pair of rubber gloves and starts washing dishes. I've seen it many times before, and I've come to recognize it. I can see someone else moving far behind her in the living room, but I can't make out the details. If all is going according to plan, it's my target.

The man is facing the woman from the living room, and it looks like he's saying something. The wife doesn't turn her eyes away from her dishes, nor does she respond. I see the husband put his hands on his hips and gesture with his hands as he says something else, but the woman keeps her gaze steady. She has been washing the same plate for nearly a full minute. Finally, the man moves into the kitchen, and at the sound, the woman jerks her head a little toward him, but doesn't look at him directly.

The husband comes into view, and I see clearly that this is my target, there's no mistaking him. The face I committed to memory is the face I see now, shouting at the woman at the sink. She tries her best to avoid eye contact, but he steps forward and leans around the counter to force her to look at him. She's on the verge of tears. His face isn't even red. It looks angry, but otherwise, there's no sign of intense emotion or being flustered.

This is natural for this man. He moves his arms wildly as he shouts, and I see the woman wince in a way I'm all too familiar with. I feel my jaw tighten and my glare bore into the home, watching the scene unfold. Whenever the man isn't looking at the woman, I can see her close her eyes and try to breathe carefully, keeping her composure.

This is the only time she can let herself show this kind of stress. While the kids are around, she can't show weakness. She has to be strong for them. God knows their father wouldn't put that much thought into their wellbeing.

The husband moves to the fridge and gets out a can of beer, cracking it open and saying something else to the woman. His face has changed. He isn't shouting anymore, because he can visibly tell he has upset her. He's annoyed, but my own experience and his face tell me he isn't backpedaling or apologizing. He's pinning the blame on her. I wonder what imagined crime he's blaming her for tonight. Maybe she said something he didn't like in front of some guests. Maybe she tried to make plans he didn't agree with. She may well have just made dinner a little later than usual tonight.

It brings me back to my own childhood, and I try to block out the memories. I didn't have the luxury of basketball practice to keep me distracted from what was going on in my home. But as I watch the scene unfold before my eyes, any shred of doubt I have for Gabe's testimony about what this man is like evaporates.

Finally, I watch my target wave a dismissive hand behind him as he makes his way out of the kitchen, and there's just enough light in the living room for me to see him heading upstairs.

According to the schedule provided for me by Gabe, he's right on time.

I have to move now.

The wife continues to wash dishes intently, sniffling occasionally, while I make my way around to the side of the building. It's a large, beautiful house that suggests wealth, even out in a run-down small town like this one. I imagine the owner likes being a big fish in a small pond. Watching through a different window, I wait until the wife finishes washing dishes, pulls her gloves off, and takes a deep breath, trying to find her center. She then turns and makes her way to the cabinet, taking out a full bottle of red wine. She picks up a glass and a bottle opener from the cabinet, then heads out of the kitchen toward a downstairs bathroom, shutting the door, presumably to distract herself with a hot bath while her husband is preoccupied upstairs.

I make my way to the sliding glass doors as silently as a shadow.

Gloved hands on the handle, I slide the door open. It is unlocked, and no alarm goes off.

Just as promised in the dossier.

I hear the sounds of running bathwater from the bathroom as I make my way inside, as well as the sound of her voice on what sounds like a phone call. There's no trace of the anxiety I saw in her face in her voice now. She does a good job of hiding it, just like my mother did. I do not crouch. I glide through the home like the reaper himself, my eyes roving over the little details in the place.

I pass by some framed pictures in the hallway, hanging on the walls. There are few pictures of the husband and wife together. The few that do show them arm in arm always feature the kids in the picture as well, usually on what looks like a vacation. I see many pictures of the husband with his friends, a few of him holding up a fish on a boat, but none of the woman on her own or with friends of her own.

The closest to that I see is one of her and the kids without the father in the picture.

It's the only one where she looks vaguely happy. I can tell the difference in her eyes. It's subtle, but once you know it, it is unmistakable.

I make my way up the stairs, passing by the two closed doors of the kids' rooms. Their names are Edward and Anthony, according to the dossier in the briefcase.

I have very specific instructions regarding them.

Once I reach the door to the study, I put an ear to the door and listen for a moment. I can hear movement, but no other sounds. I reach into my holster and take out my gun, no suppressor tonight. Things aren't supposed to look too professional. I put my gloved hand on the doorknob and turn it so slowly it nearly takes me a full minute to complete the action.

Darkness greets me in the room, save for the dull white light dancing from the single source at the far end of the room.

The husband is in the room, seated at a desk with his back facing me. Past his silhouette is the light source—an open laptop with graphic pornography playing, and the sound I heard from behind the door was the sound of him massaging himself as he watches the girls on the screen. They hardly look like they're of legal age, and the site doesn't look like one of the mainstream porn sites. He has a seat of head-phones on as he listens, presumably in order to keep his wife from hearing what's going on.

She knows better than to intrude on him, by now.

I take careful steps forward, closing the door behind me as slowly as I opened it. My eyes never leave my target.

Desmond Lamar.

His name, his face, and his crimes burn in my mind, and I have no guilt on my conscience as I step forward, preparing my soul for what I'm about to do. The headphones are both a blessing and a minor complication, but I mean to act so swiftly that it will be no matter.

I hear his heavy, intense breathing as I get closer. There are trophies of his life all around the room, just barely lit up by the light from the porn on the screen. I see glimpses of plaques from his high school glory days, old novelties from some fraternity in college, and endless fishing pictures. The dossier told me just how much was stewing under the surface of all that, and between what I saw in the kitchen and the grotesque scenes playing out on the screen in front of him, I have no doubt that every bit of it is true.

I stand behind him so closely that I'm surprised he doesn't feel my body heat. There's only so long that I can tolerate the sound of this man beating his meat furiously to people young enough to be his daughter.

I reach forward and rip the headphones off his ears.

He's so stunned by the sudden silence that he freezes for a moment.

His head whips around, and in the glow of the laptop, he sees the barrel of my gun.

"This is for Edward and Anthony," I say, exactly what my contract demanded.

BANG.

I hear a scream from downstairs as Desmond Lamar's brains and splintered skull splash across the laptop screen, which still plays its haunting video. By the time the headphones hit the floor with a clatter, I'm already halfway to the office window.

I slide it open, and as quickly as I entered, I climb down from the second story of the house down to the bushes. I keep low and move fast, so fast that by the time I hear the sounds of the neighbors opening their doors to see what the commotion was, I'm already in the woods behind the house once again.

Adrenaline courses through my body, and time loses meaning. One moment I'm in the woods, the next moment I'm keeping low near a building as cars pass by, and soon, I'm back at my motorcycle, hopping on and pulling away slowly and quietly until I'm a safe enough distance that I can start driving into the distance.

I left no traces of myself behind. Nothing but a single bullet remains to prove that anyone was there, and the gun can never be tied to the woman, whose alibi will surely be the phone call she was on when I fired the weapon.

Like I've done so often in the past, I have become nothing more than the reaper, gliding through a home and leaving with nothing but another life. Another notch in my belt. Another kill.

But this time, laying low isn't an option.

I still have one more target before this contract is fulfilled.

And that one witness to handle before my mind can rest easy...to be dealt with one way or another.

CHARITY

*E*very muscle in my body aches. Every nerve is twinging as I sit pressed up against the tree. I must have been here for hours by now, just roped to a trunk, blind to the world around me.

It must be dark outside, after the hours I have been stuck here, and after the hours it took to get here in the first place, on the back of my captor's motorcycle. I have a feeling that even if I manage to take off the blindfold, I still won't be able to see much. Not this far out into the forest, where the canopy itself is so thick and impenetrable that the light of the moon and stars is kept out, resigned to the sky.

Even without the blessing of sight, my other senses are on fire. I can hear the skittering of insects, the rustling of bushes and dead leaves as small, quick, nervous animals scamper around on their instinctual paths through the woods. And beyond them, far greater and more worrisome beasts lurk around.

I am distinctly, viscerally aware that I am no longer in my own element. In the city, in the suburbs, humans are in control. They are at the top of the food chain—in fact, they supersede the food chain altogether. But out here? In the velvety blackness and the dank, dense brush? I am nothing more than a guest.

An unwelcome guest.

Plus, this is the wrong time of night for a small, blinded young woman to be tied to a tree like a slab of gift-wrapped meat for some hulking predator with white gnashing teeth. I bounce back and forth between lamenting the fact that I can't see and feeling almost relieved that I'm not able to see just how many mysterious creatures are stalking through the trees on either side of me.

I could make a fine meal for a bear or a wolf. And even beyond the simple, expected need for sustenance, I could easily become a target for a rabid fox or something. I remember one summer when I was a little kid, our neighborhood became a stalking ground for a fox with rabies. Sightings of the little orange troublemaker started rolling in. Breaking into garbage cans, lurking around backyards and front porches. The local animal control center sent out emergency bulletins to everyone's mailbox, warning us to steer clear and keep all children safely indoors or under direct supervision while outside.

That terrified me back then; the idea that a small, cute animal like that could get sick, go mad, and wander out of its own habitat and into mine with the sole purpose of causing mayhem. Or at least that's how it seemed to me. My sister Chelsea and I spent that week playing inside, occasionally sneaking to the windows to peek outside with our hearts pounding like crazy, on the off chance that we might catch a glimpse of the culprit.

We never did see him, though. Eventually, the fox was trapped and taken away, and I never found out what happened after that, but in my research about veterinary school, I can now piece it together.

I sit here wondering if I might encounter something like that out here in the woods, alone and vulnerable. I have been working at the ropes binding me for hours, wriggling and squirming, trying to break loose. My captor pinned my arms behind me when he tied the cords, so I've been doing everything in my power to wiggle them outward, thinking that if I can just get my hands free, I can figure out how to locate and unravel the knot.

In the process, I've been forced to scrape my bare

arms against the coarse tree bark, rubbing my skin almost raw. My upper arms sting like hell, and by now they are starting to go tingly and numb. That matches pretty well with my legs, which have gone to sleep from being stuck in this same straight-legged sitting position for hours.

I'm grateful that Mr. Murderer at least had the foresight to lay down the leather jacket for me to sit on, which has insulated my butt and thighs from the damp, mulchy earth. I just know it's got to be crawling with blind worms and fidgety insects, though I've been trying my very best not to think too hard about that.

I'm not especially squeamish, especially since I have been helping my mother in the family garden ever since I was old enough to carry a watering can. But the thought of being forced to sit still while bugs crawl all over me… that's a little much for even me to handle.

I'm exhausted, mentally and physically, from this harrowing and bizarre day I've had. I was already tired from almost a full shift as a maid, but adding in hiding under a bed while listening to a discussion about a real-life murder plot, clinging to my captor as I rode on the back of his motorbike, being led blindly through the deep forest, and now my hours of painfully wiggling out of my binding—it's a lot.

It would be so easy for me to give up. To just sit here quietly in defeat as I wait for Mr. Murderer to come back and… do what with me? Kill me? Stash my body in a shallow grave? Toss me into a ravine?

And that's if he even does come back for me. What if his promise to return for me was just a lie? After all, it would be easy enough for him to just leave me here tied up, to let the wild animals eliminate me. It's the tidy, lazy way of getting rid of the evidence, isn't it?

I swallow the lump of fear in my throat. I used to think my parents' fears about the world were paranoid and unfounded, but I'm beginning to think maybe they're smarter than I realized. All those times my father warned me about getting mixed up with "the wrong kind of company" come floating back to me. I always thought he was crazy. That he was exaggerating to scare me into following their strict rules. They just wanted to keep me fearful and nervous so I wouldn't leave. After all, nothing like that ever happens in King of Prussia, right? Not in our quiet neighborhood, anyway. But now I'm seeing the truth in their worries. They didn't want me to get that job at the hotel. They fought me on it, insisting that it was too dangerous. Too big of a risk.

I can't believe they were actually right.

"Come on, Charity," I murmur to myself,

surprised at how hoarse my voice sounds. I suppose it makes sense. Right after my captor left me here, I started screaming again. I was desperate for someone to hear me. But it was pointless. I gave up. I've been silent for hours, too petrified and overwhelmed to even think straight while I listen to the sounds of the forest getting louder as the woods come alive at night.

But now something is changing. I have managed to get my arms out from behind myself. They're at my sides, the rope still strained over my elbows, but now I can finally reach up to tug down the blindfold!

It takes a few seconds for the strength and feeling to return to my arms, and as soon as it does, I bend my head and reach up with my tingling hands to pull the handkerchief off my eyes. I can't get it up over my head so I drag it down my face to let it rest loosely around my neck. I blink rapidly, seeing stars... But my elation is short-lived as I realize that even though my eyes are definitely open now, I still can't see. The stars are simply my eyes adjusting to sight once more.

The darkness of the forest is too dense to see the real stars.

I begin to pick at the rope, slowly regaining sensation in my fingers. I know the knot must be around the back of the thick tree trunk. No point in stretching to untie it—it's beyond my reach. Still, I'm encouraged by the small victories, and I hurriedly fumble around the ground for something sharp or pointy to start scratching at the cords around me. It takes me a few minutes to find a stone with a sharp edge to it. My heart skips a beat and I start to feel more optimistic and determined as I rub the sharp rock against the rope at my hip, careful not to drop it and risk losing my only shot at freedom.

At first, it seems to make no difference. The rope is thick, meant to withstand serious abuse. But I keep at it, too stubborn to give up. It takes me forever, probably a good hour of awkwardly dragging the sharp edge over the rough, slowly relenting fibers of the cord, before I see results. Or rather, feel results. Hope surges in my soul and I pick up the pace, even though my hand is cramping and my wrist hurts. Finally, with a little yelp of triumph, the cord splits!

My hands are trembling as I rush to shrug free of the ropes and fumble to my knees. I know it's probably not a good idea to try and stand up yet. My legs are still tingly and my body aches. Besides, I can't see a damn thing. So I start fumbling around, slowly stretching my arms and legs to bring the strength back to my limbs.

"Ouch," I whimper. A pang of incredible agony streaks through my body, up my legs all the way to my shoulders, and I all but collapse on the forest floor. I lie there for a moment, feeling defeated. A tear prickles up in my eye and rolls slowly down my cheek. This is a level of fear, sadness, and fatigue that I have never known before. It feels like my entire body is just on the verge of giving up on me, urging me to just rest and wait for whatever cruel ending fate has in store for me. I can feel the muddy earth cool and damp against my cheek, my forearms sticky with mossy dirt.

I wish my cardigan had long sleeves, just to protect more of my skin. And this skirt is the exact kind of clothing that is not conducive to surviving being lost in the woods miles and miles from any semblance of civilization.

I don't even like these clothes. They're outdated and overly conservative and I don't see anything like them in those fashion magazines I read in secret.

My whole life, I have been dressing and carrying myself and living my life according to what my parents want, rather than following my own desires and my own path. As I lie here on the mucky forest floor, I make a solemn promise to myself that if I manage to somehow survive this strange and frightening episode of my life, I will finally stand up to my folks for real.

I'll tell them exactly how I feel about these knee-length skirts and crew-neck tops and grandmotherly cardigans. If I ever get the heck out of these woods, I'm going to finally work up the courage to walk into a shoe store and buy a pair of strappy high-heels.

Even if I never find an excuse to wear them, I'll walk around in them at home. I'll look at myself in the mirror and finally find something about my appearance that I like. Something that's mine. My choice.

But first, I have to survive.

Reaching up to rub the locket charm around my neck for comfort, like I always do when worried or scared, I slowly bring myself up to my knees again. I brace myself against the rough trunk of the tree with my free hand, letting my wobbly legs gradually strengthen. Once I feel a little more steady, I begin to rise, still clinging to the tree for support. It strikes me once again just how dark it is here, without a single human-made light source or even the light of the moon.

Finally, I'm standing, albeit a little shakily like a newborn fawn. I tilt my head back and blink up at the canopy, letting my eyes adjust to the incredibly low light until I can just barely make out the faint shadows of leafy branches swaying gently in the breeze overhead. And behind that, the inky black night sky, dotted with soft glowing stars like freckles between the clouds.

There's no moon in sight. No wonder it's so dark. A foreboding voice in my head begs the question: did my captor intentionally choose a moonless night to carry out his plot?

"No," I say aloud, shaking my head at my own query. Of course he didn't. That would be ridiculous. Besides, from what I can tell, I was never meant to be a part of his plan. I'm just an unfortunate by-product. Collateral damage.

I was simply in the wrong place at the wrong time.

"Damn it," I murmur. "The first time in my life something exciting happens to me, and it's getting kidnapped. Bullshit."

I freeze up, stunned at how easily the swear word came rolling off my tongue. I have a split second of panic before I remember that my parents aren't anywhere around. They didn't hear me curse. I could almost laugh at how silly and crazy I must look right now. Cursing to myself, then getting paranoid that some judgmental elder might pop out of the dark underbrush to scold me for it.

Boy, I really need to get my priorities straight.

First of all, I have to figure out a way out of these woods in the darkness. I wish I had my phone, but

Mr. Murderer confiscated it and put it in that stupid briefcase. I wrack my brain for a solution, but come up empty. Well, I can't just sit here and wait for dawn. I have no idea what time it is, and besides, I don't want to be a sitting duck for predators—or worse—for my captor to come back and find me here.

Surely whatever he has planned for me is not ideal.

So, with great trepidation, I start shuffling away from the tree, hoping that I'm going in the direction we came from. I'm too blind and afraid to take big steps, so I just trudge along, my arms out in front of myself as I wade through darkness. I don't get very far before I trip over what I think is a log, and go tumbling to the ground with a yelp.

I land flat on my butt, and for a moment I'm discouraged, until I feel around and realize that what I tripped over is not a log—it's something leathery and square-shaped. With a pounding heart, I run my hands all over it, making a mental picture in my mind's eye.

"Oh goodness," I mumble, realizing it's the brief-case. Maybe it still has my phone inside! To my dismay, the case seems to be locked shut. But I'm determined.

I get to my feet and lug the briefcase with me

back toward the great tree. Summoning all of my strength, I fling it against the trunk again and again, hoping to shatter the lock somehow. To my amazement, it actually works! The whole briefcase springs open and a rain of papers and cut-out articles go fluttering down to the ground, along with my cell phone. I pounce on it immediately, my fingers shaking as I unlock the screen.

"Crap," I grumble. I have no service at all out here. But at least I can use my phone for a light. I flip on the flashlight app and shine it all around me. The light doesn't penetrate very far, only a few feet, but it's a major improvement to the pure darkness I was in before. Now I just have to watch the battery life and get out of here before my phone dies and I'm plunged back into darkness again.

But first, I'm a little distracted by the other items in the briefcase. I kneel down, using the light to read over the articles and notes. It takes me a minute or so to realize that all of this information centers around one man, who lives hours away from Philadelphia in the small town of Sheffield. Is that where we are?

What's more: this guy is a complete dirt bag. There are accusations of and arrests for counts of child luring, explicit photos of minors, underage pornography, abuse—it's a nasty portrait of a sick, evil man. Every arrest ends with a sealed plea deal.

It dawns on me that this must be the man Mr. Murderer is out to kill. I feel a little conflicted. On the one hand, this twisted man sure seems to deserve serious punishment. But on the other hand, does he really deserve vigilante justice?

Does he deserve murder?

I decide that's a moral quandary to think about once I get my butt out of this forest, so I push the papers back into the briefcase and get back to my feet. Holding my phone out in front of me to light the way and grasping the briefcase in my other hand—I want to bring proof of what happened to me tonight—I start running.

I assume I'm going east, but I can't be sure. I uninstalled my compass app ages ago to make room for secret 'what would you look like in makeup' apps. Had I known I was going to be kidnapped by a contract killer, I likely wouldn't have cared so much what shade of ruby lipstick would suit my skin tone.

Too late for regrets. All I know is that if I keep running long enough, surely I will find a way out of here eventually. It's all I've got left to hope for.

I don't know how long I've been running. Could be minutes, could be an hour. Even with the light from my phone, I'm so disoriented, watching the battery indicator drop further towards dead. My chest is heaving, my legs aching and threatening to collapse underneath me. My lungs feel like they're on fire as I struggle to fill them with oxygen, gulping down air with desperation. My legs are scratched by the underbrush, my sensible shoes causing blisters to form and my ankles to strain as they keep getting suctioned by the mud.

But I'm going to make it. I'm going to be the survivor.

I can hear the news reports changing in my head. No longer is it poor Charity Rivers who walked to her death and was too stupid to live. Now, I'm Charity Rivers, survivor. The girl who got away from her killer kidnapper.

I'm hardly paying attention to where I'm going, my eyes watering from the wind blowing into them, my vision blurring. And then out of nowhere, I run smack into something large and hard, which knocks me right back onto my butt. I look around, confused and stunned, thinking I must have somehow hit a tree. Until I grab my phone and pick it up, shining the light in front of me.

My eyes go wide and I gasp with fear, my heart sinking.

It's not a tree.

I have run right into my captor.

Charity's small frame collides with me with all the force of a wadded-up newspaper being thrown at my chest, and she bounces off with about as much grace. Before I can react, she falls hard on her ass, shining eyes looking up at me in terror. In the white light of her cellphone flashlight, I can see the fear in her face, and if it weren't for that, it would have almost been funny.

My blood is still racing, fueled by adrenaline from my latest kill. There's no blood on me to give it away, no trace of the deed being done, nothing but the mental scar of another life snuffed out by my hands.

I can justify the death. I can say it made the world a safer place, and I believe it did. I can say that in the checks-and-balances of the world, the death of that scumbag was a net positive. And I can confidently say that the people in his life will be happier with him gone.

But his death is still on my hands, even if his literal blood is not. I made sure to check myself over as soon as I stopped my motorcycle. I knew Charity was going to be scared, so I wanted to do whatever I could to lessen that.

Of course, looming over her with my wild eyes and body of steel probably isn't doing much good in that regard, right now.

Somehow, in the course of an evening, I went from cold blooded killer to concerned kidnapper. Maybe I am no better than my victim, able to change at a whim. I've always hoped to grow up better than my stepfather, but maybe his mark on me was inevitable.

She tries to crawl away from me, but I step forward slowly and calmly, my long legs making it easy for me to close the distance between us. I stoop down and reach out to take her hand. She tries to jerk away from me, and I raise an eyebrow.

"Planning on spending the evening on the cold ground?" I ask. She glares at me, jaw tight and eyes shimmering. I know she can sense the energy around me, radiating off my body like a drug. It's the adrenaline. I swear it's contagious. I can't get enough of it.

When I'm fresh from a kill, I feel like I'm high for hours afterward.

The two things I'd like more than anything right now are a woman in my bed and a drink in my hand, but neither is an option...no matter how much more *real* Charity seems to me now. I remind myself it has to be just the adrenaline high, but as I clasp her smaller hand, I can feel the warmth and softness of it, and it's electrifying.

I pull her up on her shaky legs and help her get stable, brushing off the dirt on her clothes before she pulls her hand away from me as if I burned it. She glares at me accusingly, with that same mix of fear and defiance that haunts me.

"You..." she starts, but the next moment, the defiance in her face gives way to the fear, and she takes a step back, her voice quivering. "You did it, didn't you?"

"Charity..."

"I can see it in your eyes," she breathes, putting a hand to her mouth.

While she panics, I stoop down to pick up the two items she dropped when she bounced off my chest: her phone and the briefcase. I pocket the phone and put the briefcase under my arm, giving her a cocky smile.

"I was wondering if you'd get this open," I say.

She doesn't need to know that I had forgotten about it until halfway back from the job. "Smart girl. Don't worry, I know you didn't get a call out. Not all the way out where we are." I try to make my words as calming and matter-of-fact as possible, but the edge to my voice is unavoidable. I feel primal and powerful, and that bleeds through my every word and movement.

She looks horrified that she didn't think to grab her phone before I did, and the look of despair on her face as I tuck it away is heartbreaking. She thinks she has lost everything, and the only question is what she plans on doing next.

I reach forward and brush a stray lock of hair out of her face, her skin so soft against my rough fingers. I step closer, but as soon as she realizes what I'm doing, she pushes my hand away and takes a step back to mirror me. I chuckle, narrowing my eyes at her.

"Did you read the files?" I ask, patting my briefcase. "You went through all the trouble of getting it open, and I was gone for more than enough time. What did you read?"

"Nothing!" she blurts.

"Liar," I say casually. I take another step forward, and she mirrors me again, moving backward. "You're clever enough to free yourself and get through the locks on my briefcase, so you're clever enough to do some digging. You saw his file, didn't you?"

"You *did* do it," she breathes, her voice getting shakier. "You killed him. You left me here and went and killed him, you murderer!"

"You saw what he did," I say firmly, confident that she did exactly that and knows everything I know about my target. "Are you a fan of that kind of person?"

"It was *murder!* How do you even know it's all true?"

"I saw it with my own eyes, Charity," I say. By now, she has begun to back up, and I follow her slowly, never making any sudden movements but never stopping, either. "I saw the way his wife winced away from him when he spoke. I saw how he shouted her down. I saw the misery in her face and the callousness in his. I saw the signs around the house, Charity. I saw what he was looking at on his computer, something that I'm sure you saw he was let off with multiple times. I don't trust the dossiers either, but I know from what I saw that he was responsible for every single item on that paper and more. Much more. How long do you think it would have been before his wife couldn't have taken it anymore? How long before he went too far and there *was* a murder?"

We cleared nearly ten paces as I spoke, feeling my blood racing faster. I would admit to being a criminal, even a killer, but I would not let myself be called an unjust killer. I believed every word I said. But the further we went, the more terrified Charity looked. Her eyes had grown wider, and she threw more glances over her shoulder.

I know what's coming next.

I do nothing to stop it.

As soon as I finish speaking, Charity turns and runs in the direction she came.

She's quick, I'll give her that. Quicker than imagined when I wondered about having to chase her down through the woods when I was on my way over here. But in that skirt, there's only so fast she can go, and these woods are dark.

Far darker than the suburbs we left hours before.

I take off after her.

It would be simple enough to run her down, but I don't want to send her into more of a panic than she's already in. She needs to settle down on her own, if that's what it's going to take.

I don't run at my top speed, but I keep up with her, calling after her as she runs.

"I saved his wife's life, Charity!"

She doesn't reply. She darts off the path, to my surprise, and tries to weave through a deer trail leading through the brush. She nearly stumbles when her skirt snags a branch, but she just pushes on through it and barrels forward. My thick jeans are better equipped to handle it, and I have no trouble keeping pace.

"His kids are safer now than they were with him!"

"You killed him for money!" she shouts back. I frown as I run after her, watching her dart down into a valley and trying desperately not to trip and fall. The fact that she has kept her footing this long surprises me in and of itself.

I don't have a response for her words, though. I do, but it's much more than we could ever shout back and forth like this. I don't take blood money just to buy new parts for my motorcycle or furnish my bank account. It has never been about that, and it never will be. I have my reasons, and I know that they're good ones.

I wish I could explain that to Charity. It would make things so much simpler. But it isn't the kind of thing you can sit someone down and have a discussion about. I haven't even told my own mother.

Charity reaches the bottom of the valley and races southward as fast as her legs can carry her, moving in that skirt. But she's flagging already. A sudden burst of energy doesn't last long, even in a panic. She knows there's nowhere to go, too. She might not be thinking it, but the panic is setting in. She went to a darker part of the woods, and she lost the path. She's probably frustrated at herself for letting herself get this far out. Especially now that I have her phone, and the once source of light she had been relying on.

I decide it's time to bring her back. I've let her tire herself out, but I'm not going to let her do something stupid like run off a cliff. I think she's smarter than that, but in the dark, when fear grips you so tightly you have nothing to do but run, anything is possible. You lose control of your better judgment, and unrefined instinct takes over.

I've been there.

I know what she's feeling.

The distance between us is no more than about thirty yards, and once I decide to close the distance between us, it doesn't take long for me to catch up to her. She gets a second wind as she realizes that I'm gaining on her. She screams and tries to run faster, but her flats aren't doing her any favors.

She hangs a right around a hiker's trail we've stumbled on, and the next thing she knows, she's face to face with a large boulder, and I cut off her exit. Before she can dart away, I swoop in and corner her against the stone, putting an arm against it to keep her pinned in. She presses her back to the rock, looking up at me with gleaming eyes and a fearful face. It wrenches my heart painfully, but she has to understand, if we're going to be spending any time together.

The smart thing to do would be to kill her.

She is a witness, and she does not trust me. She hates what I am. She fears me. She is a liability in every possible way, and I can't blame her for that. If I were in her life, I might well do the same. But I have to calm her down.

She doesn't deserve this trauma, and I will not harm her.

"Charity, I'm not going to hurt you," I growl, despite everything about the way the scene looks telling her the opposite. "You're going to get yourself killed if you keep running like this."

"You'd like that, wouldn't you?" she snaps. "Just another hiker lost in the woods, easy to explain away."

"You're definitely making that option easy on me," I admit, a chuckle brewing in my throat, "but if I wanted you dead, you'd be dead already. You don't strike me as a bad person, Charity, so I know you can listen to reason. The man I killed deserved it. The rich like him, the types you clean rooms for every single day for no more thanks than a low wage? They never face consequences. He never would have faced consequences for anything he did to his wife or his kids. You saw that. You saw how many times he got away with his sick crimes. This was the only way he could face justice."

"For money," she retorts, tears now streaming down her eyes in small, thin trails. I clench my jaw.

I hate that she's right. I hate that she's tugging at the strings of doubt I thought I had long under control.

"Would you rather they be left alone, free? Unchecked?"

"What makes you think you can decide who deserves to die?"

"I'm the only one who will!"

The glare between us lasts so long that I become aware of the sounds of owls and bugs in the distance, the soft din of the night relatively undisturbed by our antics. There is so much more depth to this girl's eyes than I gave her credit for.

"You are brave, you know that?" I growl, letting my arm down and giving her a little space to breathe. "Not many people would try to argue down a man they *know* just took a life."

"So you admit it," she says, sniffing as tears continue to run down her face. I stare back at her, and finally, I nod slowly, giving her a definitive answer.

I've never admitted to anyone what I was, outside of clients. No one in my life knew the real me. Certainly no woman. My heart thuds heavily in my chest, the pain of opening up to her tasting almost metallic on my tongue.

She hugs herself, clenching her eyes and letting her knees buckle as she sinks down a few inches, leaning against the boulder for support. This can't be easy for her. To go from a mundane life to this in the span of just a few hours...it's beyond reality. Today was supposed to be a normal, boring day for her.

I had the benefit of being prepared to walk this path. In that way, she is stronger than me, even. Every step of the way, she's been smart. Waiting for her exit. Waiting for the right chance to escape me.

So why does fate keep throwing us back together?

I step forward and wrap my arms around her, letting her sob into my chest. She tries to pull away at first, but she must have decided that even a killer's embrace is better than none, so she resigns herself to me. I stroke her and try to calm her down with soothing words, and after a few moments, her sobbing slows, and she is still. I let her stand on her own, and we look at each other in a new light, knowing exactly where the other stands.

"I can't leave you," I say, and I can tell she understands the finality in those words. "So I need you to come with me."

"I won't help you kill," she says.

"You won't have a drop of blood on your hands," I say, "but this contract isn't over. You saw the dossier. You heard the contract. There is one more man as evil as the last who needs to die. And I'm taking you with me."

"I'm a hostage now, aren't I?" she says in a quiet, soft voice touched by her tears.

I shake my head slowly. "That's not my plan. I'm going to be attending a party. A ritzy one. It might look strange if I show up on my own, so I have an offer for you that will let you keep some of your freedom."

She watches me carefully, and I can tell she's listening to every word I say.

"Pose as my wife," I say. "You did fine on the way out of the hotel, so I know you can handle this. Pretend we're a married couple so that I can get into this party and blend in as well as all the others. We'll need to put on a good show, but I will guide you."

Her mouth falls open in surprise. She's speechless for a few moments, then gives her head a light shake and stares at me as if trying to be sure I really said what I said.

"And if I refuse?" she asks.

I take a deep breath.

"Well," I say, extending my hand to her. "You can choose to do things the easy way...or the hard way."

CHARITY

A flash of bright white lightning streaks across the dark sky above us, and seconds later, the rain begins to fall.

My captor tightens his grip on my hand as he pulls me along behind him through the dense woods. Thunder crackles ominously overhead, matching up with the turbulent storm of emotions rolling through my mind. I am so exhausted, beyond the point of having any fight left in me. I feel as limp and useless as a rag doll as Mr. Murderer leads me confidently out of the forest, seeming to know exactly where he's headed.

I wonder if he's one of those weird people who can navigate by the positioning of the constellations and stuff. But without the moon visible in the sky, how can he possibly know? Raindrops bounce off of my exposed arms and dampen my hair, rolling down my scalp and cheeks, dripping off the end of my nose.

I think back to catching a glimpse of myself in one of the hotel room's mirrors.

I'd been dressed in my itchy, starchy maid uniform. Stray locks of chestnut-brown hair had shaken loose from my bun to hang frizzy and free on either side of my face.

My eyes had stared back at me, roughly the color of honey. My snotty little sister likes to call them "the color of dead grass," and I almost snort at the memory of the last time I saw her. My full lips and a slightly upturned nose, symmetrical dimples, and a light smattering of freckles over my cheeks and the bridge of my nose. I looked plain. Invisible in a world of famous models and actresses, my skin untouched by makeup or color.

Would that be the last time I ever caught sight of my reflection? Will that be forever how I see myself? As a lowly, tired maid, exhausted from hours of scrubbing toilets and making beds?

Of course this night has to turn rainy and stormy. It's not bad enough being tied up in the woods by a real-life murderer. No. It's got to be bad weather, too.

Part of me wonders if he's leading me to some well-hidden murder cabin where he's going to string me up and kill me. I could end up on one of those true crime documentary series my parents never let me watch. I could have my own episode, explaining the gruesome details of my misfortune.

I'm definitely back to Charity Rivers, the charity case.

That would make a good name for a true crime podcast...

But sure enough, as we keep walking, the density of the trees lessens over time, getting clearer. Finally, we walk up to the motorcycle, leaning patiently against a big bush of brambles. My captor turns to me and says softly, "Let me help you get on."

I hesitate, biting my lip as the rain pours down over the both of us.

"Where are you taking me now?" I ask, folding my arms over my chest. He's let go of my hand, but I know better than to try and make a break for it. He's at least a foot taller than me, with long legs and powerful muscles. He would overtake me in an instant, and I would risk making him angry. But what I can do is defy him in little ways. I can ask questions. I can make sure he knows beyond a shadow of a doubt that I do not want to be here with him. I can't fight, but I can be feisty.

"Somewhere safe. And dry," he adds, gesturing broadly to the rain falling.

"Safe?" I repeat incredulously. "Like I'm ever going to be safe with you."

He takes a step toward me, but not an aggressive one. He says gently but firmly, "Listen, Charity. You're much safer *with* me than without me, believe it or not."

"I'm going to go with *not*," I retort, scowling at him. "You're a murderer."

"Yes," he agrees readily. "I am. But I don't kill indiscriminately."

"Oh, sure. You're a murderer with standards," I snap, surprised at my own ferocity.

If I didn't know better, I'd say a flicker of a smile crosses his face. Then he grabs the leather jacket and drapes it over my shoulders with a touch of gentility that actually stuns me a little bit. He reaches for me, and I flinch away, but he scoops me up effortlessly and sets me on the seat of the motor-cycle. Again, it's as if I weigh less than a feather. Wordlessly, he climbs on in front of me and starts up the engine.

"Hold on," he instructs, and as hesitant as I am to put my arms around him again, I know it's my only option. I slip my arms around his waist and the motorbike pulls a sharp turn, whipping around and rumbling away through the trees, kicking up a trail of mud behind us. The bike pulls out onto the road and we drive along at top speed, toward a destination unknown. To me, at least.

I shiver, goosebumps prickling up on my arms and legs from the rain and cool night wind. We're on a secluded highway, and it's miles and miles before I see any sign of human life. Gradually, through the veil of heavy rain, I begin to notice street signs and the occasional building. Finally, I read a sign indicating that we're heading toward the Pittsburgh area. My heart twinges with fear as it hits me just how far from home I am.

My parents must be worried out of their minds. I usually come home by five or six in the evening, depending on which bus I catch. It's been hours and hours since that time came and passed. Surely they have already filed a missing person's report or started a search party or phoned the President or something by now. I can just picture my mother crying in the kitchen while my father shouts at the 9-1-1 operator on the phone, my six little siblings terrified and confused. I feel sick to my stomach imagining the stress they must be under right now.

It takes a little while for us to come across a quiet motel on the outskirts of a small town unbelievably called Climax. It's supposed to be The Redbank Creek Motel, but the neon sign flashing out front is missing several letters. Mr. Murderer pulls the motorbike into the lonely parking lot, cuts the engine, and helps me off the bike. Gripping my hand in one and the briefcase in the other, he leads me under the awning and toward the front desk.

There's an old woman dozing at the counter who wakes up with a snort when we walk in. She looks bewildered at first, then annoyed when she realizes she's been woken up. She narrows her eyes and gives the two of us a disapproving onceover.

"You're dripping all over the carpet," she remarks.

"Yes. We are. It's raining outside," Mr. Murderer replies, with surprising patience.

"Can I help you?" the old lady sighs.

My captor slides a one-hundred dollar bill across the counter to her and says flatly, "We'll take any room you have available. I don't need the change."

The old woman smiles faintly, her mood lifted by the big tip. She grabs a key off a hook on the wall and tosses it to him. He catches it and she says curtly, "Room 23. Second floor."

"Thanks," he replies, nodding to her. He pushes the door open and I follow out after him.

"Enjoy your honeymoon," she calls out sarcastically after us as the door swings shut. Mr. Murderer chuckles to himself as he leads me up the stairs to our hotel room. He fits the key in the door and we stumble inside, the lights flickering on dimly with a faint buzzing sound. There's a musty smell here, with the bed looking stiff and almost dusty. Like it hasn't been touched in a while.

The hotel maid in me twitches, going over everything and mentally tallying the things that need cleaned and changed.

But then my eyes focus on the centerpiece of the room: there's only one bed. I turn to look at my captor with horror, but he seems to read my mind. "You take the bed. I'll take the floor," he assures me. "But you might want to shower off first. Get yourself warmed up."

I nod, then frown suspiciously. "You're being nice to me. Why?" I ask.

He shrugs, peering into my soul with those bright green eyes. "I have no reason not to be nice to you, Charity. I won't hurt you. You can trust that."

I decide that for now, all I can do is accept his assurance. Without another word, I go into the tiny bathroom, lock the door, strip off my damp clothes, and climb into a warm, comforting shower. I can feel the dirt and grime and stress washing off of me, and I take my time. He still has my phone, so it's not like I can make a secret call.

Soon, though, I get tired of standing there, and I switch off the faucet. I towel off and then put on the threadbare old robe hanging on the back of the door, trying not to guess how long it's been since it was last washed.

That's the problem with being a hotel maid. You become way too intimate with the cleanliness of a hotel room.

I come out of the bathroom and regard my captor warily. He's piled some blankets on the floor like a sort of nest, and he's sitting there, watching me.

Not in a threatening way. More like he's curious about me.

I pad over and slip into the bed, never taking my eyes off of him. I know I'm not going to get a wink of sleep tonight. I don't trust him not to… try something. Maybe he's taking pity on me, and wanting to let me die in my sleep, without seeing it coming.

Finally, I tell him, "You know my name, but I don't know yours. That's not fair."

"My name is Jake," he answers.

"Jake? Really?" I repeat.

He smiles faintly and nods. "Yes. What were you expecting? Dracula?"

"Well, I've been calling you Mr. Murderer in my head, so 'Jake' is a bit of a letdown, to tell you the truth," I admit sheepishly. He almost laughs.

"Sorry to disappoint," he remarks, then sits up

and tosses me my cell phone. "You should give your parents a call."

"What? Seriously?" I splutter.

"I'm going to monitor every word, but you should make sure they know you're alive. And safe. You're about college-age, right?" he asks.

"Yes. Why?"

"Tell them you're staying over at a friend's house for an impromptu study session."

I wince. "They might not buy it."

"Just try. It's better than nothing," he reasons.

So, with the last remaining minutes of my phone's battery power, I make the call. Once my mother stops hysterically crying, she explains that my father isn't home—he's out driving up and down the streets searching for me. Another twinge of guilt twists my guts, but I have to lie. Jake is staring at me, watching closely. I tell her the bottled excuse he gave me, and of course, she has a thousand questions about it.

Before I can give a better explanation, the phone dies.

"At least that's something to hopefully calm their nerves a little," Jake says. "You should try to get some sleep now."

"Mhm. Yeah. Sure," I agree. But I spend the entire night only dozing in and out of sleep. Every time I start to drift off, I jerk awake to continue staring at my captor. And even though he's lying down with his eyes closed, I know he's not sleeping either.

THE NEXT MORNING, Jake gently prods me awake and offers me some freshly-laundered clothes. It takes me a few minutes to come to terms with my strange surroundings.

I have never spent a night away from my family. Even growing up, I never had sleepovers. Not even with Aubrey, who was next door. If we wanted a sleepover, she stayed at my house.

So waking up in a musty motel room with a strange man who—oh yeah—is my kidnapper and also a murderer, is a bit of a shock. But I sit up, still wearing the ratty old robe, and the events of the last twenty-four hours come trickling back to me.

"I got up early to wash and dry your clothes at the motel laundromat," Jake says. He's already fully dressed and seemingly refreshed, although the dark circles under his eyes and the stubble on his jaw beg to differ.

"Oh. Um. Thank you," I reply, startled by the strangely considerate gesture. I plod into the bathroom and change back into my old clothes, this time eschewing the cardigan. I come back out and lean against the sink counter, staring at him. Jake has a cup of what looks to be crappy hotel coffee in his hand, sipping at it gingerly.

"Come with me," he says, beckoning for me to follow. I raise an eyebrow.

"Where are we going now?" I ask.

"Shopping," he replies, as if it's the most obvious answer in the world.

"Wh—what? Shopping?" I repeat, confused. He nods and opens the door, letting bright sunlight filter in. "What are we shopping for?"

"New clothes. No offense, but you can't wear that outfit to the party," Jake remarks as I reluctantly follow him down to the parking lot. Just like always, he helps me up onto the bike, and he ignores my stammering questions all the way along the highway to the next bigger town, which seems to be a suburb of Pittsburgh—an upscale one.

I'm still bewildered when he parks the motorbike and leads me into a cutesy shopping district, holding my hand and smiling as though we're just a happy couple on a road trip. I remember that that's supposed to be our cover story, and I hastily slap on a smile of my own. We walk into a little boutique of fancy, beautiful, handmade formal gowns and handbags.

No one would believe that the handsome, young

man is my kidnapper. That Mr. Murderer—— Jake—is a murderer. We look *far* more like a cute, mismatched couple out to go apple picking than a hostage and kidnapper looking for a cover for a murder.

"What are we doing here?" I hiss into his ear.

"Go get yourself a dressing room, okay? I'll bring you some dresses to try on. What size are you?" he asks.

I blush. "I-I don't know. Honestly."

Jake gives me a look up and down. "I'll figure it out," he says, and leaves me to wander into a dressing room, aided by a cheerful attendant who seems to have no idea that the two of us aren't a happy couple. I stand in front of the mirror, looking at my bedraggled, unbrushed hair and makeup-free face, suddenly feeling self-conscious. Moments later, there's a knock at the door and I gasp in fear.

"It's just me. Try these on," says Jake, and he heaps several long, glamorous dresses up over the door.

They are... gorgeous. Nicer than anything I've ever owned, and far closer to my forbidden fashion magazines rather than my conservative closet.

I open my mouth to protest, then think better of it. No use in arguing. This may be a fever dream, but it's also real life. I pull the dresses into the dressing room and try them on one by one, each time stepping out to show Jake. I have never worn dresses like these before. Plunging necklines. Exposed backs. Spaghetti straps. Strapless. Sequined and sparkly. Slits all the way up to my thigh. I feel so out of place at first, but with every new look, Jake compliments me, his eyes drinking me in as though I might actually be a girl pretty and worthy enough to wear these gowns.

And even more surprisingly, he seems to be totally genuine about it.

I suppose to be a contract killer, you also have to be a very good liar.

Finally, I step out in the last dress: a long, gorgeous black gown with a slit up one leg, thin straps that slip off my shoulders, and an unholy amount of cleavage. Jake stands up, his jaw dropping when he sees me. He looks me up and down slowly, nodding his head and smiling.

"Yes. This is the one," he says softly. The attendant claps her hands excitedly and rushes off to the cash register. Jake walks up to me, looking totally in awe. I can feel my cheeks blushing bright pink.

"I still don't understand why we're buying a dress," I mumble.

"So you can wear it to the party tonight. As my wife," he adds, smiling, his finger running along my jawbone and sending a thrill of something forbidden down to my core. "Don't worry. It's all part of the ruse. But honestly… you should own this dress anyway just because it looks like *that* on you. Charity, I'm sure you hear this all the time, but you are beautiful."

Feeling conflicted, I reply weakly, "Actually, no. Not really."

"You are full of surprises, but that is the biggest one yet," Jake remarks. "Your parents must keep you at home all the time."

I nod, stunned at his accurate guess.

"Yes. That's exactly right."

"What a pity," he muses, looking down at me with genuine affection.

I change back into my street clothes and we purchase the dress, which turns out to be about as expensive as an entire semester of classes. I'm still gob smacked by the price—and by how effortlessly Jake paid for it—when we get to the next shop.

This one is a jewelry store. It doesn't take me long to figure out why we're here. If I'm supposed to be Jake's 'wife' it only makes sense for me to have a wedding ring. Jake is nothing if not thorough with his murder disguises, I'm learning. We play the part of a happy couple, wandering around hand-in-hand, cooing over pretty gemstones and diamond rings until we find one that truly makes my heart skip a beat. It's a modest but elegant pink diamond offset with two tiny white diamonds on a rose gold band. The shop assistant takes it out of the case and Jake slides it onto my finger. To our mutual surprise and delight, it's a perfect fit.

"It's like it was made for you," Jake murmurs, and once more, he sounds... genuine. Like this isn't just a game to him. As if I'm not the cover for his crime.

I don't know if it's the lack of sleep, the mesmerizing shiny diamond, or just good old-fashioned Stockholm Syndrome, but my heart is fluttering as though this is all real. Like we're really a happy couple picking out a ring together. I keep trying to snap myself out of it, remind myself what kind of situation I'm really in here, but I just can't shake off the feeling that this is fate. I feel giddy. I feel like I could float away on cloud nine. And Jake is feeling it, too. As the shop girl is wrapping up the ring at the register, Jake pulls me close. With my heart pounding so hard it hurts, he leans in slowly and kisses my lips. Sparks fly. My whole body seems to be on fire. I have never been kissed before, and even in my wildest dreams, I never imagined it could feel *this* good. Somewhere in the back of my mind, alarm bells are ringing. But right here, right now, in this bizarre little bubble of reality, I feel good. And I can't think of anywhere else I would rather be.

It's crazy.

It makes no sense at all.

But Jake's lips pressed against mine, his hands gripping my waist—it feels right.

Am I losing my mind?

er body trembles in my grasp, and the feeling of her delicate lips against mine is so sensitive that I can feel every twitch in her as we kiss.

I wasn't expecting her to return it. It was just supposed to be for show, and I couldn't even dare to hope that it could become something... more.

Yet she pushes back towards me. Her lips don't just accept my touch, but they touch back, pushing into mine as her muscles slowly relax in my grasp. I can feel every shift in her body, and I know the difference between a polite gesture and the real thing. Charity is surprised at what I did, but she isn't faking.

If she is, she's a better liar than me.

The soft sound of our kiss breaking is followed by

the briefest of stares shared between us, but it hints at so much more than I was ready to handle when I leaned down to kiss her. My hand squeezes her hip a little more firmly, and she doesn't pull away. We're both stunned by what we've done.

I can't deny that it has felt good to spoil the girl a little this afternoon. I wasn't expecting to enjoy it as much as I have, but the simplicity of making her smile makes my heart beat faster. She doesn't deserve to be caught up in my world, and I know how I feel about her. Maybe it was my sincerity in that kiss that made her step her game up.

Maybe I'm just seeing things in my head.

But no, the look in those eyes is genuine. I would know it anywhere.

Will it be a blessing or a complication for the rest of the night?

"Ahem," comes the clerk's voice, and we snap back to reality. Charity's cheeks go bright pink, and she looks away from me, pulling away from my hips ever so subtly. I let her go, turning to the clerk and giving a smile as cool and casual as if the kiss had never happened.

After seeing the total, I take out cash to pay our tab. I don't fail to notice Charity's eyes widening at the sight of the stack of bills I use to pay, and even the cashier is a little surprised by such a show of wealth. I imagine she mostly deals with credit cards, or at least installment payments. But it was all cash that I have been given for preparation for this job. As far as I'm concerned, this is just another one of those expenses.

Once the bill is settled I smile down at Charity and offer her my arm. She takes it, but she avoids making eye contact with me. I pretend not to notice as I give the cashier a quick, grateful nod as we're thanked for our business, and I lead her out of the store without another word.

Several minutes of us walking pass without any further conversation. The sounds of our shoes hitting the ground is all that we hear over the sounds of the street, and the way back to the hotel is just as terse. If I hold a door open, she thanks me briefly with a smile, and if I guide her this way or that to keep her out of the flow of foot traffic, she complies without resistance, but something has changed.

I steal a glance at her as we make our way through the hotel lobby, and I see that her face is remarkably without expression. She looks forward, and her cheeks are still pink, but she seems too wrapped up in her own thoughts to do more than react to the world around her. What can I say? Nothing in life ever prepared me for a situation where I accidentally share a genuine kiss with a woman who's supposed to be a small step up from 'hostage'.

I can't let myself get distracted from this job.

While I do think the money spent on Charity was money well placed, I'm starting to run low on the cash I have for mission prep, and at this point, there is no room for error. I can't afford that, either in terms of my budget or my success rate. Everything has to go flawlessly... even though I'm tied to an amateur who shows some promise.

As we get into the elevator and it starts to take us up to our room, I start to wonder if she's letting the pressure get to her. Maybe this is too much for her to handle. I would be surprised by that, but something is clearly bothering her. It's almost funny, thinking that of all the things that could break the camel's back about posing as a hitman's wife, a genuine kiss would be the one thing to throw her off her game.

I can't blame her. Anything can happen, if you aren't prepared for it.

But as we step into the room with nothing said between us since I held the door open for her at the jewelry store, I know I can't let this go unaddressed. The hotel room door closes behind us, and I follow Charity to the bed.

I decide to take the direct approach. I toss the bags down in a chair, then take Charity by the hips and spin her around. She looks into my eyes in shock for a brief moment before I press my lips into her again, and this time, I hold her there, my hips against hers, nothing to intrude on us.

In here, we're not on stage. There's no one to perform for. There is simple, private, honesty.

She tenses up. I feel every muscle in her body going stiff, unsure what to do, but she doesn't pull away. Does she fear me even here? Even in this? I squeeze her hips, but she doesn't relax. Finally, I pull back from her and look down at her searching eyes.

"There," I say in a low, husky tone. "Is that what was bothering you?"

"What do you mean?" she asks, but she doesn't move a muscle.

"Ever since we touched in the shop," I say, "you've been tense. I can feel it."

"You must read me pretty well, for someone who's only known me a day."

I crack a smile.

"You learn to read people, in my way of life. And you never answered my question."

Her eyes look down to the floor for a moment. She's trying to come up with something. Anything. But she isn't as practiced a liar as I am, and she already has enough on her mind with everything else going on today.

"Charity," I whisper, "I need you to be relaxed if we're going to pull this off. People who are jumpy make mistakes."

"How can I *not* be jumpy?" she asks, half-smiling at the ridiculousness of my statement. I nod understandingly, but I walk her backward until we're at the edge of the bed, and I slowly sit her down. "You realize what you're asking me, right?" she pleads with me and my heart pangs. I don't want her in this situation any more than she does.

"I do," I say calmly, and I bring a big, rough hand to her knee, squeezing it and moving it slowly up her thigh. Our eyes are locked, and she seems to be almost trying to read my mind to see if I'm really about to do this. "But I have ways of making you relax."

Her cheeks burn a brighter red, and she looks down at my hand. Her hand twitches, and I know she was about to put it over mine. I stop, still reading her face.

"You can tell me no," I say clearly, and she turns to meet my gaze. She might not be an experienced liar, but she is good at masking her emotions when she wants to. She looks confused, but there is so much more in those deep eyes that escapes me. "But if you don't, I will do what I want to you."

The only change on her face is the growing red in

her cheeks and I slowly push her onto her back. She hesitates for a moment, as if she doesn't know what to do with herself. Almost unconsciously, she slides her shoes off, but her eyes are on my pants, watching the growing bulge between my legs.

"No," I say, reaching out and tilting her chin up so that she can face me. "We don't have time for that. Only my mouth."

She looks confused for a moment as I push her further back onto the bed, coming after her inch by inch. "Me... to you?" she asks, pointing from her mouth to my cock, and I shake my head, chuckling.

"That wouldn't help you relax much now, would it?"

She looks like she's holding something back, but her face is filled with anticipation and wonder. I can't help but imagine that she has never had this done to her before.

I suspected that she wanted this, even hoped she did. I think she's so surprised at the fact that it's happening that she isn't even sure how to respond. But we don't have time to think, only act.

If she didn't want this, I'd simply do a shot of whisky with her, but I have her attention now.

She doesn't resist as I push her back and run my hands up her bare thighs, bunching her skirt up above her waist and revealing her underwear within.

There's so much wrong with this. I am her captor. She knows what I'm capable of. She ran from me, and she's only cooperating now because...why, exactly? I can't help but wonder if the kiss we shared in the store has something to do with how she's acting now. She watches me carefully, propped up on her elbows as I glare at the thin fabric separating me from her pussy, almost curious to see what I'm going to do next.

It would be wrong of me not to oblige her.

I reach in and pull her panties aside just enough to expose her pussy, and I see the faintest hints of glistening wetness in her swollen folds. I smile, feeling self-satisfied. I was right. The moment we shared earlier set her thoughts in motion. I didn't take her for the type, but something in her seems to like our time together. Maybe Charity will have a few surprises in store for me yet.

But first, I need to give her hers.

I reach up and grab her hips as I move forward on the bed, feeling her eyes watching me with more anticipation by the moment. She wants this, but she isn't sure how to proceed. Could this truly be her first time getting touched by a man's mouth, or is she just being cautious around me. Either is possible. She knows what I'm capable of. She knows what my body can do, when I use it to do harm. She is sheltered. Her mannerisms and her clothes tell me that much. But a sheltered person isn't immune to the kinds of thoughts that make even experienced people blush.

I push her skirt up further and breathe in the scent of her needy, ready pussy. It fills my body with energy and drive. I crave her and everything she has between her legs. I want to hear the sound of her voice, to help coax out all that desire I sense she has bound up inside her.

My rough hands run up and down her exposed inner thighs, savoring the feeling of them as I watch her body, seeing her chest rise and fall. We're both clothed, and I suspect Charity isn't even thinking about the possibility of taking her shirt off. That almost makes this more enticing. Neither of us left the hotel room today expecting this. Hell, we didn't even sleep, we've been so suspicious of each other.

This is one way of burying the hatchet, I suppose.

I couldn't be more pleased.

Clutching her hip in one hand and holding her panties aside with the other, I lean in and let my tongue stroke over her pussy in a quick, soft motion. She gasps immediately as if touched by fire, and I feel her try to close her legs, but I hold them open. Still, I raise my eyes to hers and give her a cocky smile.

"Are you sure you want this?" I ask.

She looks down at me, breathing hard, but the desire on her face is written as clearly as words in a diary. "Yes," she says, "I...I want it. I want you."

I lunge in again, and I let my tongue pass over her pussy more fully, wetting the outer lips. The taste of her is better than I could have expected. Her honey fills my senses, from the warm touch to the heady scent to the taste that makes me hunger for more. I dig my fingers into her further as I start letting my tongue out in soft, gentle strokes across her lips, getting a little deeper with each stroke. I'm almost sure that this is her first time at this by now, even though she's trying to play it cool, and I want to ease her into it.

Finally, I start getting further past her outer lips, stroking the most private parts of her that only she has touched, probably in what she thinks are moments of weakness. The guilt heaped onto women for enjoying their own bodies is shameful. I hear the sheets crinkle softly as she grasps them with her hands, and I glance up to see that she has let her head fall back as I get deeper. I've barely gotten started, and she's reacting as if we've been teasing each other all afternoon.

Something about that makes me feel good deep down, on a level I very rarely get to access. I hold back a smile as I keep licking her, and at long last, I let the tip of my tongue brush up against her clit.

I have to hold her thighs open again as she yelps, and her head jerks up to look at me with wide eyes. I don't acknowledge her. I tighten my grip and push her thighs open, crawling further onto the bed and taking more of her into my mouth. My teeth brush against the sensitive flesh above her clit as I start tormenting it with my tongue, and the further I go, the wetter my face gets.

Five o'clock shadow is starting to show across my face, and it brushes and scratches her lips gently as I eat her out.

"Oh my gosh," she breathes, her voice nearly cracking. The subtle weakness she shows makes my cock throb and pulse between my legs, and I desperately wish we had time for me to relieve myself more in her.

That will come. Now that I've tasted her, I know it's inevitable. I'll have her again. But for now, I want to give her something entirely new.

The long strokes of my tongue become brushes on a canvas, and as her rapid breaths get so loud that I can hear them, I revel in her. My tongue dives as deep into her as I can plunge it, and I take my time in dragging it up all the way to her clit, flicking it teasingly before withdrawing and starting over again.

She starts pushing her hips up into me, letting out soft whines and desperately urging me to give her clit more attention. But every time she tries to time her thrust just right, I draw back, not giving her clit more than a flicker of hope each time.

It doesn't take long for her to get truly desperate. Her hands on the sheets twitch a few times. I know what she wants to do, but she's nervous. This is definitely her first time doing this. Probably her first time being with a man.

What does that make me?

Am I truly the monster deflowering this girl after kidnapping her? She's trying to hide it—is she self-conscious? That kind of thing would never bother me, but in fact, with Charity, the idea excites me even further despite myself. I crave her more and more as I realize how innocent and untouched she is, and I grow even more commanding, holding her hips down and taking complete command of the situation.

Her sharp breaths soon become steady whimpering, and her hands finally jerk up, reaching out to run her fingers through my hair and clutch my head. She tries to push me into her, but I hold fast. She's my victim now, utterly at my whim. I can deny her an orgasm as long as I want.

And god, I draw it out longer than I would for

anyone. It's unkind, I know, but the sounds coming from Charity's lips are as sweet as the honey coming from her lower ones. My face is doused, and she squirms and writhes in my grasp with awkward, clumsy motions.

"I...I feel tight," she whimpers, a hint of worry in her voice. That's when it clicks beyond a doubt that I'm dealing not only with a virgin, but with one who may well have never had an orgasm before—not one like this, at least.

I let my thumbs stroke her, and I give her reassuring squeezes even as I hold her down and subject her to my sweet torture. My tongue is unrelenting, and indeed, I feel a change in the way her pussy quivers to my touch. I'm driving her toward her orgasm faster than she could ever have expected.

It's my responsibility to guide her through it.

"J-Jake!" she gasps, wide eyes looking down at me in fear as I drive her to the brink. "Jake, I- *ohhhh goodness!*"

Her sharp cry fills the room and makes my cock throb as she comes in one strong, full-body orgasm that wracks her to the core. As she tries with all her might to clench her thighs and push my tongue away from her clit, a jet of fluid squirts out from her and hits me in the face, dousing me in more of her honey as she convulses in my hands.

"What- I- oh gosh, Jake!" she whimpers, eyes closed and cheeks bright red. I give her soothing, approving groans in reply as I start lavishing her pussy with long, gentler strokes, guiding her through the orgasm with all the experience I have. Over the course of nearly a minute, she twitches and squirms on the bed, and at long last, when it comes to an end, I release her and look up at her with a face glistening with her fluids.

"I-I'm so sorry!" she gasps, seeing my face and looking so genuinely afraid that I can't help but laugh. "What's funny? Stop that!"

"You're adorable, for your first time," I growl, crawling up to her so that I can reach her face. I wrap a hand around the back of her neck and press a kiss to her lips, letting her taste herself on me. She moans softly into the kiss, and as if she hadn't already melted enough in my hands, the kiss renders her a useless pile of jelly on the bed.

"Was that...what was that?" she asks, pointing to my face. I turn my head to laugh again, and she bites her lip and slaps me playfully on the arm. "I'm being serious!"

"It's called 'squirting'," I say, stroking her hair, "and it's perfectly normal. Not everyone does it, but it just means you...well, really enjoyed it. Your body did, at least. But what about the rest of you?"

She breathes a few moments, looking delightfully messy in my arms before smiling softly, too over-whelmed to do otherwise. "I...yeah, I liked it a lot." I grin and give her another kiss, rubbing her thigh before breaking away and going to get a towel from the bathroom to clean her up.

"Good," I say in a husky tone as I return and wipe her off, carefully replacing her panties and smoothing her skirt out. "If this evening stresses you out, just keep that in the back of your head."

"Wait," she says, looking worried. "How did you know I'm...or *was*...?"

"That this was your first time?" I say, toweling my face off with the same towel and flashing her a smile. "Don't worry about it. Not everyone would count that as your real 'first time', but I don't care about labels. I certainly enjoyed myself," I add with a wink, and her cheeks redden again for a moment before she turns her head and smiles.

"Regardless," I go on, tossing the towel aside, "now's not the time. Get dressed." I check my phone's clock, then hold it out to her so she can see the time. "We're late."

$\mathcal{I}$ bite my lip, standing in front of the mirror in our hotel room, wearing the long black gown Jake bought for me today, wondering how the hell I'm supposed to make this all look natural. During our shopping excursion today, the two of us stopped into a beauty shop to buy makeup and hair products, and luckily Jake seems to have an eye for this kind of thing.

Of course, it helped that the attendant at the store there was eager to give me a brief tutorial on how it all works.

She even gave me a quick mini-makeover (which she unfortunately wiped off before I left the store) to show me the basics. The woman must have thought we were an odd pair: this rugged, devilishly handsome tough guy in a leather jacket with a girl who looks as though she just broke free of a nunnery or some conservative boarding school. When she asked me what kind of makeup I usually wear, I truthfully admitted that I have never put makeup on in my life.

Her eyes went wide and her jaw dropped, as she was apparently unable to imagine that in this day and age, there are still women who go au naturel all the time. I was embarrassed, so I quickly added that on one occasion, my friend Aubrey secretly met up with me in a girls' bathroom on campus after class to put lip gloss and a light coat of mascara on my face.

Even that had scared me to the core, as I was terrified that somehow my parents would find out and punish me. It was enough of a push to convince them to let me attend classes, but if they found out I tried on makeup at school? Well, I worried that would be the unceremonious end to my academic career. But the shop attendant seemed only more excitable about my makeover once I explained that I was a makeup virgin. I suppose she doesn't come across that opportunity very often in her line of work.

Staring nervously at my bare face, with a tube of shiny mascara clutched in my hand, I think to myself, *I've lost my virginity in more ways than one today.*

I glance at Jake in the mirror. He's already dressed for the event, after having left to collect the car he's renting for this evening. He's sitting on the bed, pointedly not looking at me. He's on his phone, giving me a little privacy to work on my look. I still feel giddy and disoriented from the magic he worked on my body earlier.

I don't understand how he was able to make me feel...like *that*. I have only touched myself a few times in my life, and it never turned out the way it did with Jake in control. In fact, it's never felt particularly good or rewarding when I was by myself. It's strange. I know very little about sex, admittedly, except for what I've sneakily read in magazines or heard second-hand from Aubrey.

Most of the sex tips I gleaned from my covert research has led me to believe sex is more about pleasing your man, about making yourself as smooth and skinny and pretty as possible. It's about being alluring and interesting—giving him a taste, but then pulling away before he can do everything he wants to do. It seems like the only pleasure a girl is supposed to have is whatever happy by-product occurs in the commission of his pleasure.

An orgasm (a dirty word, according to my upbringing) for a woman is just a stroke of luck.

Unnecessary.

Unproductive.

It's all about him.

Women are meant to orbit their men. A moon to a sun.

And the way I was raised certainly has never proven to oppose this idea. I mean, I have always expected that eventually, I will be married off to some strong, silent, imposing man who will tell me what to do and provide for me. I don't have to make big decisions. I don't have to reach very far. I've always been told that it's best to keep my desires small and accessible. Easy things like a shared home, a shared car, some children, a kitchen to cook in.

Maybe permission to occasionally go to the movies unaccompanied or something. Don't want for much, but don't ask for much either.

And for years, I've always kind of accepted that. After all, that's how my mother lives, or seems to. She is stern and assertive with my siblings and me, but when my father is in the room, she wilts like a flower, turning to him for guidance and permission. Still, they seem to love each other, and I've never known anything else. I've always kind of based my ideals of a marriage on what observations I've collected from watching my parents interact.

It doesn't look especially exciting, but it's comfortable, I guess. That's something. A little stability in a world of frightening horrors and the vast unknown lurking beyond your front porch is a welcome thing, right? And if that means sacrificing my pleasure, my comfort, my lofty desires to get that little dose of predictability, it's worth it. Right?

But over the short period of time I've spent with Jake, he's shown me a different world. One that is somehow both scary and intriguing. I find myself less threatened by him and more curious about him. It's not often one gets the chance to see a villain up close and personal, and now that I'm here—as up close and personal as one could get—I'm starting to rethink my assumption of him as a villain in the first place.

I mean, the teachings I grew up with would beg to differ. He's a killer, and that should automatically mark him as a Bad Guy. Or so I've been led to believe. But then, so far he's only killed other bad men. Worse men. Unforgivable men. So, is it really a net loss? I'm finding that the simple, black and white, easily categorized world I imagined is an inaccurate image. It's not that easy. There are shades of gray between the white and black, and when you squint, you can find all sorts of wild, unexpected lives moving in every direction in the cracks.

Jake lives inside a shade of gray. I can see that now. The rules of society, at least as I've learned them, don't seem to fully apply to him. He takes the law into his own hands. He holds himself to a different set of standards than I'm used to. And now that I'm being carted around alongside him, maybe I'm inside that gray space, too.

"How's it going over there?" he asks suddenly, jolting me out of my thoughts.

"Um," I hesitate, blushing. "It's not going at all."

"We don't have a lot of time," he reminds me gently.

"I'm worried I'll do it all wrong," I confess with a sigh. "I-I've looked at makeup in magazines, and those dumb apps. I tried to follow along with what the shop girl explained to me, but I'm still scared. What if I try it and it looks terrible?"

I can see Jake turn to look at me and smile in the mirror. "You'll be fine. You can figure it out, Charity. I believe in you," he assures me. "Just give it a shot."

I swallow hard, nodding. I take a deep breath and lean in closer to the reflection to start applying a modest layer of black mascara to my long lashes. It takes me a few frustrating tries to get it to stop clumping together messily, but finally I get the hang of it. I grin at my face in the mirror, impressed and proud of myself for getting there.

Gathering up my confidence, I then apply blush, highlighter, fill in my eyebrows a little darker, and put on a brightly-pigmented red lipstick. It's not the most technically-perfect makeup job, but it looks similar enough to what I've seen in magazines.

Next, I decide that the easiest thing to do to my long brown hair is just to braid it. Luckily, I have younger sisters, so I have lots of practice French-braiding.

It's just another small way to pass the time when you're cooped up in a house all day. I get a little fancy with it, using one of the many superfluous hair products to make my hair sleek and smooth, then creating a French braid over one shoulder. Lastly, I slide the brand-new sparkly ring onto my wedding finger and nod approvingly at my reflection as Jake sidles up behind me.

"Damn," he murmurs, leaning in to let his warm breath tickle my ear. He kisses the side of my head, letting his powerful arms draped around me.

"Does it look okay?" I ask nervously. *Why do you care what your kidnapper thinks of your looks, Charity Rivers?* I hear my inner voice hiss at me, and I try to push it out of my mind.

He chuckles softly, sending a pleasurable vibration down through my body. He looks at me in the mirror with a grin. "Charity, it looks way better than okay. You look fantastic," he says.

I giggle and turn away, embarrassed. "I'm not used to this. Any of this," I admit. He takes my chin in his hand and tilts my face up. I can tell he wants to kiss me again, and that thrills me to the core, but he stops himself, not wanting to mess up my lipstick.

"Get used to it," he growls, those green eyes flashing with… desire? "Tonight, you and I both have to play the part. A wealthy young power couple attending a gala."

"I'm worried people won't buy it," I murmur.

Jake's phone dings and he glances at it. He offers me his arm, and I take it.

"Don't you worry about a thing. Fake it 'til you make it. It's time to head out. Come along, gorgeous," he says with a wink. I feel warm and tingly all over, torn between shock, panic, and excitement. I don't know what he has in store for me beyond tonight. If someone had told me that I'd be willingly, excitedly attending a social event with my roguish captor tonight, I never would've believed it. But things change. And the way I feel about Jake tonight is a complete reversal of the fear and distrust I felt last night.

We head downstairs, taking the elevator, and get into the sleek black car. During the long ride to the event, I lean into Jake. I know, logically, I should still fear him. And perhaps deep down a small part of me does. But although it makes no sense, I trust him. I feel safe with him in a way I can't really explain. He makes me feel whole. He makes me feel… real.

And in his eyes, when he looks at me, there's a softness. The occasional flicker of something akin to regret, like he feels bad for giving me an ultimatum before. Is it possible that he's starting to grow fond of me? It seems impossible but, then again, all of this is insane already. What's a little more surreality on top of it all?

Finally, the car pulls up to a massive estate, passing slowly through a gigantic wrought-iron gate. The mansion looms impressively over a gigantic lawn of topiary animals and expertly-manicured gardens. The house itself is easily over five thousand square feet, and it looks like it could swallow my parents' house whole. Jake brings the car to a parking space between two other luxury vehicles obviously belonging to party guests, and we get out by the marble front steps. Jake locks the car, pockets the keys, and then we head inside with a nod to the dignified doorman. I can scarcely breathe as we walk into the lavish home.

As soon as we step inside, I can hear the echoing swells of live jazz music coming from deeper within. We walk down a long corridor with a vaulted ceiling, stained glass windows on either side. Tapestries and paintings I recognize from my textbooks hang on the walls. There are marble statues and a few mounted family crests that look to be older than the country itself. The music and chatter of the crowds grow louder as we approach the main great hall. My lungs feel tight and my head is dizzy, but Jake gives me a comforting squeeze, which helps me relax.

"Don't worry," he whispers, "I've got you."

And suddenly, my worry melts away.

We walk into the great hall and my jaw drops at the unfathomable opulence surrounding us. The room is filled with well-dressed guests chatting and laughing over glasses of wine. Waiters in black suits weave through the crowds carrying silver trays of champagne flutes and crudités. To one corner, there is a live band playing upbeat jazzy music, and there are some people dancing. Two staircases curve up to a second floor with a balcony in the center that over-looks the festivities. This place looks like a film set and feels like a cathedral. It's difficult for me to process the idea that someone *lives* here.

"Is this... is this real?" I ask breathlessly.

Jake chuckles. "Yes. It is."

He molds himself to the occasion, taking on an air of opulence and casual luxury himself as we move from gathering to gathering, mingling and chatting breezily with other guests. It stuns me to see how effortless this transition is. Jake morphs from motorcycle-riding, leather-jacket-wearing badass to soft-spoken, confident, formal man-of-the-hour with ease.

His confidence is contagious, and before long I find myself warming to the occasion, laughing and chatting as though I belong here. It's exhilarating, this kind of extended roleplay, and after a little while—and after my very first glass of bubbly—I'm even having fun.

"Nice to meet you. I'm Jason Hawthorne, and this is my wife, Charlene," he introduces himself to a pair of middle-aged couples in tailored suits and designer evening gowns. I have to stifle a giggle at the made-up pseudonyms he conjures up for us. We all shake hands.

"My, my, you are just darling!" gushes one of the women, an older lady with a pearl necklace and frosty white curls.

"Oh, thank you!" I reply, trying not to get flustered. I'm not used to all the flattery.

"Isn't she beautiful? Would you believe she did her own makeup?" 'Jason' says.

Both women gasp and exchange expressions of wonder. "Goodness. I never would have guessed. It looks downright professional," compliments the other lady, who has dyed-red hair in a straight bob and bright green eyeshadow. A colorful feather plumes artfully from her fascinator cap. I find myself thinking that she looks a little like a peacock, but in human form.

"Do you not do your own makeup?" I ask them honestly.

They both titter between themselves, as though I've asked the silliest question in the world. Jake pats my arm reassuringly.

"Oh no, dear," says the white-haired woman. "I have a makeup artist on retainer."

"And my nanny moonlights as a makeup artist, so she does mine," answers the peacock.

"Nanny?" I repeat, warming to the subject. "You have children?"

The peacock lady glows happily. "Yes, yes. Two of my own, both grown by now. But I also have three adopted children. They're four, six, and nine. Lovely children."

"That's so nice, adoption!" I exclaim genuinely. "I'm sure they love having siblings to play with, too. I have six younger siblings myself."

"Six?" gasp both couples. Jake gives me another little squeeze, and this time, I realize he's trying to warn me.

"Yes," I answer with a smile. Then I divert away, asking, "What are your children's names? Do they get along well?"

The conversation wanders on easily, the women

chatting with me while the men swap hunting stories with Jake. I wonder vaguely if Jake has ever been hunting or if he's just an adept liar. Then I remember that he has gone hunting, in a way, but not for animals.

Finally, the conversation dies down and Jake politely says goodbye to them and leads me away. He leans in as we leave the area and says softly, "You might want to be more careful about handing out personal information like that, Charity. If you give away too much, you might be identifiable. And that would make me identifiable, as well."

I wince, my stomach churning.

"Oh no. I'm so sorry. I didn't even think about it."

He smiles gently and gives me a kiss on the cheek. "It's okay. This is all new to you. I don't expect you to be perfect. You're doing an amazing job," he says.

I smile in spite of myself, my cheeks flushing pink.

"I'm trying."

We continue on in similar fashion for what seems like hours, drinking champagne and mingling with the vapid, wealthy guests. Jake often gushes about how he's the luckiest man alive to be married to me, complimenting me and discussing my made-up achievements. I know it's all for show, but that doesn't keep me from enjoying it. I'm actually smiling and laughing, having more fun pretending to be 'Charlene Hawthorne' than I've ever had as Charity Rivers.

I don't know whether that's proof of how intoxicatingly pleasurable it is to spend time with Jake, or if it's just a testament to how boring and dull my life was before. Either way, I'm making the most of the evening, getting dizzy and giddy from champagne and proximity to Jake.

Out of the corner of my eye, I notice some figures appear at the balcony of the second floor, and I point it out to Jake with a tipsy grin. "Who're they?" I slur in a whisper.

His smile fades as he turns to look at them, and I feel his body stiffening up beside me. Suddenly, I'm worried. "What is it?" I ask.

There's a man in a suit, standing with a beautiful woman who seems to be his wife. But behind them are two other men—much bigger and bulkier, less opulently dressed. If I didn't know any better, I'd think they were bodyguards.

"Something isn't right," Jake murmurs, watching them hawkishly. He leads me away to a quieter corner, never letting his eyes drift away from that balcony. I don't know what's wrong, but the tone of the evening is quickly shifting into something totally new and frightening, and all I know is that I want to stay close to Jake. With him, I am safe. That much I know.

But when one of the bodyguard's eyes scan the room and lock onto the two of us, my blood runs cold. Jake's right. Something is off, and I have a feeling that our pleasant evening masquerading as a happy couple is coming to a swift, ugly end very soon.

As soon as the two body guards' eyes land on us, as seamlessly as if I'd been planning on doing so before they even entered, I turned to Charity and kissed her. She let out a soft murmur of surprise, and I brought my hand to her chin to hold her there a moment as I savored her lips again. My heart pounded harder, despite the situation. I bent her at the waist, leaning into the kiss so hard that I felt a few of the people around us watch, an approving chuckle coming from some of them. Charity was starting to have a lasting effect on me.

I needed it.

When I finally break the kiss, she blinks at me with confusion in her eyes, cheeks blushing. "What was that for?"

I lean in close to her ear and whisper, "No reason,

I just wanted to taste your lips again, since this isn't the best place to taste your other ones."

Her blush goes deeper. Watching her sparkling eyes get shiny with wonder makes my cock throb, and if I weren't on a job, I would already have her halfway to the nearest private room to make good on that desire. Hell, if this were a lesser job, I might still do just that.

But a face worth $500,000 just appeared at the top of the stairs with a small army of bodyguards, and I need to think carefully about what's about to happen next.

"Are you always like this?" she asks, smiling and quirking a brow at me as I get us moving slowly again.

"Like what?"

She tries to fight off the smile on her face, and she glances away for a moment, blushing, and I can't help but chuckle.

"A little more forward than some of the men you've been with? Maybe not on purpose, but yes, I think I am," I say smugly.

She giggles, and I know she's thinking *which men?* That's good. We should keep it light and easy between us. I need to keep her from getting too involved in the mission at hand. If her mind is focused on less serious matters, she's less likely to crumple under the pressure of our precarious situation. Meanwhile, my own mind is fully trained on the task in front of me.

It's Gerald Callahan, no doubt about it, and his young wife about half his age. He's the kind of man who gives out so many fake smiles I don't think he knows how to give a genuine one. He can smile with his eyes well, even though it's all a sham, and the cameras eat it up. As a state politician running for office and a friend and partner of my last target, he's every bit as much of the same scum as him. The world will be a better place without him, and I don't have a scrap of remorse for what I'm going to do tonight.

But security is everywhere. As Gerald starts smiling and handshaking his way down the stairs to mingle with the guests, I see security start to make its way out after him. I glance around us to the other exits and entrances of the building and see that the ones coming out with him aren't the only guards he has. The security detail is coming out in full force, and I know the look in their eyes.

They move from person to person, occasionally following lone men with steely eyes, occasionally speaking into their headpieces and communicating with each other. They're pretty well organized, and I spot more than one captain among them.

Word must have spread very quickly for my target to have this much security beefed up already. That complicates things. But they're not expecting my ace in the hole: Charity. A lone man like me walking around this place would have been tackled and escorted out already. It might have made local news, and my target would have been regarded as a hero and probably had a better time with the election coming up because of it.

But Charity makes me almost invisible.

She carries herself well in a place like this. Like me, she doesn't seem to come from money. We haven't talked about ourselves hardly at all, but women from affluent society usually don't take jobs as maids at local hotels, no matter how nice the hotel may be. The way she walks and stands doesn't draw attention to herself. She has dignity, but she doesn't seem like she's looking to make waves. Her beauty can just breathe on its own, her rich brown hair hanging past her shoulders in a luscious braid, and her warm eyes drinking in the evening's good cheer.

In other words, she's a perfect cover.

The bodyguards are looking for a lone man. They aren't looking for couples.

"Let's get you another drink," I whisper, and I tug Charity toward the nearest server. As we go, I start scoping out potential places to make the shot I need.

There are a thousand factors to consider during something like this. I can't risk hitting anyone else, which is a fine concern to have, in a room absolutely packed with people dressed similarly. My target reaches the bottom of the stairs and quickly forms a small circle of other socialites to start chatting and schmoozing, and a server brings them all glasses of champagne in an instant.

As we get to a server of our own and I get a glass for Charity, I wonder if any of my target's suck-ups and acquaintances have any idea what a horrible man he is behind closed doors. He did an incredibly thorough job of keeping his first divorce under wraps, thanks to a hefty alimony that kept his ex-wife quiet about the bruises he gave her. It was even enough to keep his children in therapy. I have a feeling my last target's inheritance will leave his wife and children with enough for the same.

The music's airy, dreamy lilt carries through the room as Charity looks around with growing anxiety in her eyes, and I can't help but check in on her every few seconds as I look around, trying to seem inconspicuous. Watching my target without looking like I'm watching him is even more dangerous now that there are guards searching for a man who's doing exactly that. If I'm caught staring at the target too much, even Charity's presence won't hide me.

And that's not the only thing I have to worry about tonight.

I notice Charity watching my target, and I remember that she has seen his face in the dossier. She knows exactly who he is and what I plan to do. Her eyes turn to me for a moment before she busies herself with a long drink, eyes turned away from me. I clench my jaw, knowing there's nothing I can talk to her about regarding all this right now. There are too many ears around.

So, if she wants to blow my cover and save my target's life, she has the chance now.

All I can do is hope she sees reason.

I fully believe everything that I told her when I was first talking her down in the woods. These men deserve to die, and they'd almost certainly never face justice if they were allowed to roam the world freely. They aren't the first to live happy lives doing heinous evil deeds, and they certainly won't be the last. But if I can put the fear of god into some of these rich assholes, maybe that will change their tune, if only for a short time.

Soon, I notice that people are starting to turn, and I follow their eyes to my target, who is now standing in a semi-circle of his peers and clinking a fork to his glass to get everyone's attention.

"Ladies and gentlemen, thank you all again so

much for being here," he says in his usual smooth voice and friendly candor. "Let's not delay things any longer—we've already missed America's birthday, so let's make up for it with a fireworks show worth the wait! If you'd be so kind, make your way in an orderly fashion out to the yard, and we'll get things started properly before dinner."

There's a mild but thorough applause throughout the room that Charity and I take part in, giving the man a smile as fake as his. I glance sidelong at Charity, who appears uneasy. I wrap my arm around her waist and draw her in to my side, smiling at her lovingly and kissing her on the forehead.

She smiles back, but I can tell her nerves are ramping up. I'm going to have to make this quicker than I would like.

Callahan and his entourage are the first to leave the main room. The guards start to clear a path gently for them. They can't be too forceful, because everyone here is the same kind of high society as my target himself, but they have to make it clear that he's still the most important person in the room.

If Gabe wants to make a splash, this is going to do it, that's for damn sure.

Once they reach the doors, a pair of servers push it open for them and let the warm air inside while they go. Outside, I can see that a real treat is prepared for the guests. There are many white tables set up for everyone on the lawn, and I can barely make out where some of the fireworks are already being prepped not far from a huge tent where my target and the guests of honor will be seated. It's shaping up to be a romantic evening, and the smell of grilled food is already wafting into the building and making stomachs rumble.

As my target heads outside between his wife and a bodyguard, I notice that some of the workers by the fireworks are getting ready to start getting the show off to an early start. It occurs to me that Callahan probably arranged it so that the fireworks will start *as* the guests are coming outside to wow them, not after.

I have to move quickly.

Taking Charity's hand in mine, I start pushing my way upstream with the rest of the crowd that starts to follow everyone outdoors. There are four guards at the doors, and I see them watching the crowds carefully. The gun I have concealed is burning a hole in my side. They're looking for me, but I have to bank on Charity keeping me from being noticed. We reach the doors, and the guards give me a glance up and down...

...and we walk through to the other side, untouched.

Callahan is saying something to his wife up ahead, and further on, I see the sparks of one of the first fireworks being lit.

It's now or never.

I clutch Charity's hand tightly and pull her to the side, making our way as close as possible to him without leaving the safety of the crowd. Everyone's attention is on Callahan and the fireworks. And when I see the wick get lit and the spark work its way up to the rocket, I finally reach into my coat and clutch the handle of my gun, silencer already attached to the barrel.

The sound of the rocket taking off is loud and sharp, so much so that some of the people in the crowd wince or duck. I hear Callahan's laugh as he watches the thing go up high into the air just as I make it to the edge of the crowd and see my opening.

The burst of red lights high up in the air is the last thing Gerald Callahan sees before my bullet flies from the gun barrel and hits him right in the back of the head at the base of the skull.

One of the guests not far from my target frowns and looks down at his clothes as he feels something spatter onto him. His mind hasn't even processed what the flecks of red on his white shirt are before Callahan's wife screams, and her husband's body hits the ground.

"Run with me," I growl into Charity's ear.

But her face is frozen, jaw hanging open, expression shocked. She's white as a ghost. She saw the entire thing from start to finish.

The next thing I know, I see her tense up, and she lets out a shrill scream that joins the chorus of other screams sounding all around us. In truth, it probably helps throw suspicion off of me—nobody is looking my way, it seems, but I can't bank on the idea that nobody saw me.

"We have to go, *now*," I hiss, giving her a tug. She looks at me, horror in her eyes as chaos starts to break out all around us. Guests start panicking, some start running or ducking, and bodyguards are spilling out into the yard, chattering into their head-pieces feverishly.

I clutch Charity's hand tight and bolt.

My instincts kick in. Like so many other guests currently losing their shit, I make a break for the parking lot, and I try to blend in with them as conspicuously as possible. If I look too professional, move too carefully, then the guards will see me as the assassin I am. Charity is running and keeping up with me just fine, but I won't rest easy until we're in the car and blazing out of here.

"Don't let go of me," I urge Charity as we hurry

through the sea of cars. I can't hear police sirens yet, but it's only a matter of moments.

The car comes into sight, and I feel adrenaline coursing through me, urging me on.

Just a little further, and I'm in the clear.

This was for you, Mom.

CHARITY

Distantly, through the thick fog of terror and shock clouding around my head, I can make out the frightened, panicked screams of my fellow party-goers. I can see their faces twisted into grotesque masks of fear, mascara-black tears tracking down porcelain cheeks. Composed, well-medicated, tipsy people from the upper echelons of elite society crying out in true mortal dread for probably the first time ever in their easy, comfortable lives. Sheltered people running for shelter.

And even though I am certainly not wealthy like they are, I *am* sheltered. I have never felt anything like this before. I have never watched a man die. Not even in the movies. My parents never let me watch that kind of thing. Besides, even if I had, there's no way a fictional death could possibly hold up to the sense of watching it unfold in real life. Watching the power and presence of a human being dissipate into thin air.

It happened so quickly. The man, whose name I can recall from the dossier in the woods was Gerald Callahan, was standing and beaming brightly one moment, his eyes locked on the burst of bright red fireworks. And the next moment, there was another shock of bright red—this time from the bullet bursting through his unsuspecting skull.

That spray of blood, so surreal and yet viscerally grounding at the same time, will surely be locked away into my deepest, darkest vault of memories for the rest of my life. A big smile, a loud crack, and then he collapsed. Like a popped balloon, he fell defeated and deflated to the ground next to his horrified wife.

There was nothing anyone could have done to stop it. Even the hulking presence of his two body-guards could not protect the bad man from meeting a cruel, but swift end. He suspected that something terrible might happen to him. He was concerned about his safety. He did what he could to prevent his own death, but it doesn't matter now. I am realizing now that if death wants you, it will take you where you stand, wherever or however that may be.

No matter how much money you have squirreled away in the bank, no matter how strong or wise or cocky or powerful you are, death can find you and take you away in an instant. A big man in life is just a bigger corpse in death. More wasted oxygen. A broader grave to dig.

I just can't seem to process how quickly it all went down. He was up and full of life, and then in an instant that life—with so many years and so much experience tucked away—was snuffed like a blown-out candle. And the worst part of it is that the man responsible for his death, the grim reaper of tonight's event, is the same man who is pulling me along by the hand right now.

The same man who kissed me and gave me pleasure beyond anything I ever could have imagined. The same man who has protected me and treated me like a princess today.

And for whom I still feel a twinge of affection. Despite everything.

What is wrong with me?

"Charity, come on!" he says urgently, tugging at my hand. Those dark brows are furrowed together in worry, his green eyes flashing, pleading for me to move faster. I'm not intentionally trying to drag us down. I don't want to get caught either. I mean, at this point, I'm more than just an unwilling hostage.

I am an accomplice. I'm the cover story. I am Jake's supposed alibi.

I know that's why he bought me this dress and encouraged me to make myself pretty, to drink champagne and chat with the other guests. I'm just here to make him look less suspicious. To lubricate the sticky situation and make it easier for him to carry out his diabolical murder plot.

And I did.

I played my role like a true actress, without fighting back at all. I gave him what he wanted, and now, as a result of my actions, a man is dead. His wife is a widow. Sure, he was a bad man and I can try to tell myself she's better off without him but... I can't know that for certain.

"Hurry," hisses Jake again, "we have to get out of dodge."

I want to pick up the pace. But my legs feel like they're made of lead. My whole body is going numb with shock, my mind drifting away to a safer, quieter place, far from the wreckage of this dramatic scene. Out of reach.

"I-I'm trying," I manage to choke out, my throat aching with a hard lump. I'm doing my best to keep from crying, until I realize that I already am. The tracks of tears on my cheeks feel cool in the night air as we move along, the breeze drying them into thin, sticky streaks.

"Wait! Nobody leaves until the police arrive!"

bellows a booming voice from somewhere behind us, breaking out over the din of screaming guests. I gasp and whip around, wild-eyed, to see one of the body-guards glaring out over the parked cars, his broad chest heaving and his hands clenched into fists at his sides. He is glancing around with crazed suspicion, and when his eyes lock with mine, my whole body stiffens up.

He narrows his eyes and his mouth hardens into a flat line as he leaps off the marble steps and starts barreling in our direction.

I scream in terror, which makes Jake glance back over his shoulder. When he sees the bodyguard coming after us, he swears, "Shit!"

He starts running faster, but I can't keep up. I trip over a rock and go flying through the air with a star-tled yelp. I close my eyes and brace myself for a painful impact, but instead, Jake effortlessly catches me in his arms and hoists me over one shoulder, carrying me off to the rental car. He unlocks the car, all but tossing me into the passenger seat before sliding behind the steering wheel and throwing the engine into gear.

The enraged bodyguard is just a few feet away when Jake yanks the lever into reverse, slams his foot on the gas pedal, and whips out of the parking space. The car peels out down the long driveway, with the bodyguard bolting athletically after us, shouting and shaking his fists.

I can't stop trembling and whimpering in fear as Jake expertly weaves the car in and out of the choked line of vehicle traffic and foot traffic along the way. There are people running alongside the car, crying and hysterical, making their way toward the front gate just like we are. Jake is glancing in the rearview mirror with a strained expression, trying to shake off our assailants. But I'm staring straight ahead, watching the wrought iron gates start to materialize out of the shadowy darkness.

And when I see them, my mouth falls open and my eyes go wide.

My heart sinks.

I gasp and reach over the console to flail at Jake's chest with my hand, breathless and desperate to get his attention. "J-Jake! The gate! The gate is closing!" I cry out. Someone in the mansion must have activated the gate's controls to close and therefore keep any and all suspects from fleeing the scene. The gates are very slowly closing, but the space through which we could fit is narrowing right before my eyes.

His own eyes flit back to the driveway ahead of us and he murmurs, "Fuck. Hold on."

He slams his foot down on the gas pedal and leans forward, dodging and weaving as other cars and fleeing guests appear out of the darkness. I clutch both sides of my seat, praying desperately while tears stream down my face.

I can't stop murmuring to myself in full-blown panic while my heart races along. "There's no way we're going to make it," I whimper. "We are going to be stuck here and the police are going to come and they're going to arrest us and we are both going to jail and my parents will be so disappointed and—"

As the gates start to wrench closed around us with a gut-twisting metallic creak, the back bumper of the rental car just barely squeaks through unscathed. Still in total shock, I whip around in my seat to look out the back windshield, gawking at how close a call that was. The gate clinks closed with a definitive scrape of metal on metal. Countless vehicles screech to a halt, trapped within the bounds of the estate while Jake pilots the car out of sight down the quiet road.

"We made it," I breathe, still shaking all over.

"Yes. We did," Jake confirms. "Close call, too."

"But you—but we—we killed that man," I whisper, tears rolling down my cheeks.

Jake glances over at me with a stern look on his handsome face. He shakes his head. "No, Charity. I killed that man. Not you. Don't carry this burden yourself," he warns me.

But I'm too far gone, the guilt rising up to swallow me whole. "I-I went along with your plan. I was your cover. I did what you told me to do and now a man is dead!" I gasp.

"You knew that was the plan from the start," he says quietly.

The emotions bubble up inside of me and I can't hold back, screaming at him, "You killed him! You killed that man right in front of me!"

"He deserved to die," Jake insists. I cradle my face in my hands for a moment, my whole body coursing with sobs. This is too much for me to process.

"Jake, you can't do that. It's a sin! And it's against the law," I counter, my words slightly muffled by my hands.

"The law is not always fair," he says.

I look over at him, horrified. "The law is the law! There's a reason laws exist. We have to follow the rules or—or bad things will happen," I murmur, feeling lightheaded.

"Bad things happen in spite of the laws all the time, Charity. That man, the one you're mourning for right now, was an evil man. A true, real-life villain. He hurt people. A lot of people. The world is better off without him," Jake explains calmly.

"That's not your choice to decide," I protest.

"That's—what is it called? Vigilante justice. You can't take the law into your own hands. It's wrong!"

"Charity, I know you think the world is black and white, but that's not how it really is. Everything is complicated. Everything is difficult. And every person has to live by a moral code. Sometimes the law can't catch up to true morality. Sometimes it's not perfect. Bad men slip through the cracks all the damn time, and if the law can't bring them to justice and make them pay for their mistakes, then someone else has to. It just so happens that this time, it's me," Jake tells me passionately.

He glances over at me, those green eyes bright even in the darkness of night. I'm shaking my head, unable to come to terms with the events of tonight.

"You saw his file, Charity. You know what kind of a brute he was," he adds.

"I just don't understand why you have to be the one to make it right," I mumble softly, looking out the window as tears roll down my cheeks. Suddenly, I just feel so exhausted. So overwhelmed. I haven't slept in far too long, and my body feels like it weighs a thousand pounds. I'm too weak to fight, but I need to keep trying.

We ride along in tense silence for a few minutes, and then Jake speaks again, this time in a low, cautious voice. "Do you want to know the truth?" he asks.

I drag my eyes away from the window, turning to look at him. "Yes. I-I need to know, Jake. I want to understand," I sniffle.

He sighs, staring hard out onto the road before us. "That man in the hotel room, the one who hired me, he is paying me a lot of money to carry out these executions," he begins.

"I know that part," I remind him. "You kill for money."

"Right. But you don't know why," he goes on, looking over at me for a second before turning back to the road. I stare at the side of his face expectantly.

"Go on, then," I prompt him.

He takes a deep breath and admits, "I need money. Specifically, I need money to give to my mother's doctors. She... she's sick. Really sick. We lost our insurance. They won't pay for her medications anymore. She needs those meds to survive. Without them—without them she can't keep going on. My mother is dying, Charity, and unless I get a lot of money very quickly, I am going to lose her."

It takes me a couple seconds to register what he's telling me.

"You need the money for your mother?" I repeat. He nods.

"She's sacrificed so much in life to raise me and take care of me, and now it's my turn to save her. We don't have the money. We don't have any other choice. The medications she takes, the ones that keep her alive while she's waiting for a transplant, they cost hundreds of dollars a day. The doctors' visits cost hundreds. The diagnostic testing costs thousands. And she can't work right now. She can't earn money—and she shouldn't have to. Not now. Not while she's just barely struggling to survive. It's not fair. She's a good woman. An angel. And yet these rich assholes get to cause so much pain and suffering in the world and nobody stops them. Nobody puts the money where it's meant to go. Nobody cares about the good people like my mother," Jake explains, the emotion in his voice making my heart surge with pity and understanding.

"But you do. You care," I say quietly.

He nods.

"Yes. It's all on me to make things right. I can't change the whole world, but I can do this small thing. I can finally punish two evil men and remove them from the world to make it a better place, and at the same time, I can save my mother."

"Two birds, one stone," I whisper.

"Exactly," Jake agrees. "I know you don't get it. I

don't expect you to. But this is what I must do, Charity. I don't have any other choice."

"No. I do understand," I reply honestly. He looks at me, surprised. I can feel myself softening, warming up to him again. Even more now that I know why he's doing this. He's not being selfish or vindictive. He's trying to bring a little balance back to this dirty world.

I think about my own mother, about how much I adore her. She's not perfect, but she tries to do right, and she's always taken care of me, even if she pushes me too hard or holds on a little too tight. If my mother was dying, I think I might do the same. I would do anything in my power to save her.

"I never expected to have someone along for the ride with me," he says, reaching over to take my hand. "It was never supposed to happen this way. I swear. I was supposed to act alone. No witnesses, no accomplices. But you just fell into my arms. I could never have predicted that. Neither of us meant for this to happen, but now that you're here, we have to adjust. I need to know if I can trust you, Charity.

"I need to get paid and give the money to my mother before the cops can catch up with me—if they ever do. But that means I have to rely on you to keep this secret and follow along with me."

"You need me to cover for you," I reply.

Jake nods, and it looks like this suggestion pains him, but he has no choice.

"Yes. I do," he admits, then turns to look at me with pleading eyes, vulnerable for the first time since I met him. The power is in my hands. I have to decide what to do with it.

But the answer is simple. I don't even have to think twice.

I give his hand a squeeze and answer softly, "I'll do it. I'll help you."

couple days later, I'm standing over a hot griddle in our hotel suite in the city of Lancaster, glancing out the window at the rapidly fading light of the overcast Pennsylvania skies. The clouds cast an ominous light over the industrial red brick that so much of the city is made of. There's a very specific kind of mood cities like this one convey, and I'm not poetic enough of a person to put it to words. I can't even decide if it's more good than bad.

The spam and eggs sizzling on the pan in front of me most definitely smell good, though.

"I...didn't think the smell of spam would ever make me hungry," Charity says, making her way into the kitchenette and getting herself a bottle of water from the fridge.

"I figured we could use some comfort food that

didn't make us feel like garbage after eating it," I said, giving her a gruff smile. "I usually don't turn my nose up at fast food, but sometimes you really need the smell of something hearty cooking in a kitchen to keep you grounded when you're on the move."

"Or on the run, I guess," she adds, and I chuckle.

"Well, I wasn't going to put it that way, but…"

We left the hotel in Climax after a hasty checkout. "On the run" was a very modest term for our state right now. We made our way east as fast as possible after turning in the rental car and getting back on my bike, and told her I dropped off our fancy clothes and the engagement ring at a charity. It was tempting to just drop everything and run without taking care of those loose ends, but that was a dead giveaway for someone suspicious. Hired guns left a trail of unfinished business behind them. Honest, law-abiding citizens followed the rules as they fled.

Local news is covering the hits more than any other story. When I walked into the store in the predawn hours of this morning to pick up the supplies we needed, I saw my own handiwork being covered on the television. That never gets old.

Still, this is the biggest splash I've ever made by far. Gabe was right. If I can survive the fallout from this bang, I could have some real clout in the criminal underworld, muscling in next to some of the biggest fish in Philly. At least, I could, if that was what I wanted.

But all I really want is to put all this behind me, take my paycheck, and fade into the shadows. That's what I've wanted since I started this whole ugly business, and the finish line is right in front of me at long last. I'm not about to make some rookie mistake and serve jail time for trying to do the right thing for someone I care about. At least, not until the money is safely where I want it to be.

"I've always heard it's good fried, but I never really tried it," she says.

"Don't make me sound like a commercial for it," I say, serving up a couple of plates as she pads over to me and looks over my shoulder, sniffing. "But I ate a lot of it growing up. I just think of it as pure protein to keep you going, minus some of the grease you'd get at a burger joint."

She takes a drink of her water as I fix her plate and hand it to her, and she carries it over to the couch and takes a seat against one of the arms, stretching her legs out over the cushions. As I watch her, I feel my manhood stirring between my legs. Being this close to Charity for the past few days has been messing with my senses. She's an incredible distraction, even if we haven't done anything since I tasted her in the hotel room before the hit. I've started to notice the more subtle things about her over time, like the way she plays with her hair, the way she shifts around when she's standing, and the inflections of her voice when her mood changes.

It's remarkable how much you get to know about someone when you're on the run with them, and it's even more remarkable when you find yourself drinking in every detail you can find about her.

Maybe it's because I've spent so much time alone the past few years. My life doesn't give me much room for a social life on the side, and besides, that would just open up a dozen more risks to compromising my identity and landing me behind bars. Charity isn't exactly what I had in mind when I would think about how nice it would be to have someone to confide in—I've never liked the idea of having to take a hostage, if I can even still call her that, and I don't even know if I can truly confide in her.

She has surprised me so far.

I banked on the nonstop, fast-paced rush of the contract killing to keep her distracted, and that worked, but the past two days have been calmer. She has had much more opportunity to make a move of her own, especially during the times when I can't keep a close eye on her.

We actually got some sleep, which is more than I was expecting.

I get my own plate and make my way over to the desk chair, taking a seat in it and cracking open a beer from the fridge.

"Sure you don't want one?" I say, nodding to the beer.

She looks tempted, but she finally shakes her head with a smile. "I'm good, I think. This is really tasty," she adds, pointing her fork at the food as she chews.

I chuckle as I dig into my own plate. "You think so? Maybe I should quit this and graduate to the big leagues, working a line at a diner."

She laughs softly, politely covering her mouth with her hand as she does, and I see a little pink in her cheeks. I know she's probably ashamed of laughing about a fairly serious subject, but she has been full of surprises each day.

"So," I say, changing the subject, "did you ever hear back from work about getting your shifts covered?"

"Yep," she says after swallowing a mouthful. "One of my coworkers owed me a favor for covering her for a bridal shower last month, and we have a new hire who's eager to get as many shifts as he can, so I should be good for a while. However long this is...you know, lasting." She seems a little uneasy at that, which is understandable. Not even I can say for sure what the endgame here is.

I wouldn't hold back anyone I trusted, but I have a lot of ground to cover before I can say I trust anyone. But letting her make phone calls has been a big step for both of us. Police haven't swarmed the hotel yet, so I can only assume that she hasn't been using the phone to call for help yet.

"And your parents?" I ask.

"I haven't heard more from them since I told them I was driving out of town for an internship interview," she says. "I told them I'd be pretty distracted the whole time, so they're giving me some space, believe it or not. I'm sure they're going to keep me under twenty-four hour surveillance if—when I come back, but for now I think we're okay. Still, that's only going to buy me a few days, so I'll have to come up with something after that, if I- if we're out that long."

I nod, thinking. "If it comes to that," I say, wanting her not to feel like she's trapped with me long-term, "you can say you were offered the internship, but they wanted you to start immediately, and they put you up in a hotel until they can get you settled in somewhere more permanent. And when it's time to go back, you can tell them the business changed hands last-minute, and they dropped the internship program."

She flutters her eyes at me in mild surprise. "Wow. Do you just come up with cover stories off the top of your head like that for fun?"

I chuckle.

"Survival tactic," I say before taking a quick swig of beer. "My stepfather was a cruel man. When I was small, I couldn't resist him physically. When I did something he didn't like, I had to either face the consequences from him or come up with something to appease him. Option Number Two left me with a lot less bruises."

She goes quiet for a few moments, looking surprised and shocked all at once, slowing her chewing down. It's a reaction I'm used to by now. I feel my stomach tighten. I don't like people feeling sorry for me, and I don't like dampening the mood.

"That's all in my past," I say with a smile, trying to keep her from getting morose. "He's out of the picture now, and my mom and I are both trying to just move forward. I wouldn't consider my skill in lying as a 'perk', but if it helps, it helps."

"Here I thought *I* had a strict upbringing," she says with a faint smile.

"What was yours like?" I ask, sitting back and leaning against the desk.

"My parents just…" She pauses, looking away for a moment and frowning. "I'm the oldest of six siblings."

"See, that already tells me a lot," I say, chuckling, and she smiles back at me.

"Yeah. I became the 'backup parent' after the third child, and it hasn't really stopped since then. And on top of that, my parents have always been pretty strict with just about every aspect of my life."

"Having to check in with them for disappearing for a few days at your age tipped me off, yeah," I say.

She rolls her eyes. "It's *always* like that. I don't get it. I've been an adult since before I was a teenager, but they still treat me like a kid, you know? One of my sisters is just sixteen, and she's allowed to run around with any guy she wants like it's no big deal, but I'm twenty-one and they still act like I need a chaperone."

I raise my eyebrows. "Wow. I can relate to growing up early, but I can't imagine being handheld that long."

"That's the craziest part," she says, shaking her head. "Growing up and slowly realizing most of your friends have way more freedom than you to do all the things you thought only irresponsible people do. One time, when I was seventeen, there was another guy in the homeschooling community who liked me. He asked me out on a date, but my parents said the only date they'd let me go on was having him come over to hang out with all of us as a family."

I cringed, giving her the most sympathetic look I could muster. "Little bit of a cockblock."

"Well," she backpedals quickly, blushing, "I wasn't thinking about any of *that*, but yeah, something along those lines. I just don't get it. My siblings act out all the time, and I'm always the one being as responsible and mild as possible, but I'm the only one my parents ever seem to come down on so hard. It just makes me feel like I'm working hard for nothing but giving them something to nitpick, you know?"

"That...sounds exactly right," I say, eyebrows raised. She pauses at that, furrowing her brow, then raising them.

"Yeah, I suppose it could be."

"I'm not the best person to talk to about parents and good intentions or otherwise," I say, finishing my food at the same time as her and standing up, "but I can relate to needing to get away. So with that in mind, I've got an idea. We've had a rough few days, and I think you've earned a break."

She stares up at me in confusion as I take her plate. "What do you mean?"

"I mean," I say, "that we should indulge some of that teenage rebellion you never got to work out."

"Oh, so aiding and abetting a contract killing isn't enough teenage rebellion?" she points out with a smirk, and I wink at her.

"I'm thinking something a little more down to earth. We passed a nightclub on the way here, just around the corner from the hotel. What do you say we go for a walk?"

She looks shocked, and she doesn't seem to know how to reply for a few moments. Her cheeks are blushing, and I get the impression that she's interested, but she'd never normally agree to something like this.

"I'll make it easy on you," I say, pulling on a jacket. "I'm going, and I can't leave you alone, so you're coming too. You don't have to drink or dance, if you really don't want to. Worst case scenario, you get to hang out somewhere new and let me buy you whatever non-alcoholic drinks you want."

She starts to stammer some excuse, but I move over to her and take her hands pulling her up to her feet and making her laugh embarrassedly.

"I mean, when you put it that way..."

"Great!" I say, grinning. "Let's get you ready. I don't think the bar is going to be very high for a club in a city of less than a hundred thousand."

✷ ✷ ✷

HALF AN HOUR LATER, I'm trying desperately not to laugh at how comically uncomfortable Charity looks on the barstool next to me.

The club, if you can call it that, is about what you'd expect from a small city. It's nothing flashy, but it isn't abysmal. The floors are sticky, and there aren't really crowds to speak of so much as a smattering of people who happen to be able to find time for a little downtime on a weekday night. But the DJ is doing a decent job of not making me feel like I've stepped back in time a few years, which is more than I can say about a lot of them.

"See?" I say, leaning against the bar and smiling at Charity. "It's not the end of the world. You're not addicted to hard drugs...yet."

"Now you're just making fun of me," she says, giggling.

"Okay, but really," I say, turning to face her and glancing at the bartender. "You're twenty-one. I'm guessing you haven't actually had your first legal drink yet?"

She hesitates, and my smile grows.

"Okay okay, let me think," I say, putting my hand on my chin and looking at her thoughtfully. "Let's go with something sweet. How did you like the champagne? Are you sensitive to the alcohol taste?"

"It was alright," she says, looking nervous but interested. I nod.

"Rum," I decide after a moment.

"What does that taste like?"

"That's not as important as what you use it in," I say. "I'd suggest a Pina colada for a starter drink, but that's not exactly a club drink. How about a mojito?"

She gives me a blank stare.

"It's minty," I explain.

"I do like mint," she offers, somewhat at a loss, and I crack a smile, getting the bartender's attention. A few minutes later, he sets a frosty mojito in front of a wide-eyed Charity, who peers at it in wonder.

"It's not very strong," I warn her. "Club drinks never are."

She takes a tentative sip, and she keeps her face unreadable.

"It's...not bad," she says reluctantly. "I can definitely taste the alcohol."

"May I?" I ask, holding out a hand, and she hands me the drink to give it a taste. "Wow," I remark as the strong taste of rum goes down smoothly. "Good bartender. That's a little stiffer than I'd start you out with, so you're good if you can deal with that."

I order the same as her, just to make her feel better

about her first drink, and we start downing the drinks while I explain the differences between white, spiced, and dark rums. She seems amused by how much variety there is, and I get a kick out of explaining basic drinks as if it's a science.

Once we reach the bottoms of our drinks, I'm not feeling much, but I can see the pink in Charity's cheeks not going away, and she's smiling more than usual.

"How's that drink treating you?" I ask, chuckling, and she flutters her eyelashes, looking down at it.

"Oh wow, I drank that kinda fast, huh?" she says, and I can't help but laugh. "What? Am I supposed to drink slower?" As she speaks, the DJ changes the song to a new track that I like, and I get an idea.

"Drink however you want," I say. "We're not driving. And we're not dancing, either—we should change that part."

"Wait, what?" she says, but I'm already standing up and taking her hand, pulling her onto the dance floor. "Oh my gosh, wait! We're not dressed for dancing!"

"All the better," I say, urging her out onto the floor. "Besides, it's not like anyone's watching."

Charity blushes furiously as I move to the middle of the floor, and despite what I said, there *are* some people watching us with mild smiles or looks of jealousy. That gives me a little pride deep within me. The thought of being seen with this sweet girl and others being jealous that I'm with her makes me happy, and Charity seems to enjoy it too, whether she's fully aware of what's going on or not.

I take her hand, and I start leading her in an upbeat, fast-paced dance in the middle of the club. She looked like the type who would be good at it, but she surprises me with how easily she falls into step, like a natural.

"You dance well," I remark after a few moments.

"You lead well," she says without missing a beat, and I grin.

"This is one thing that isn't your first, I'm guessing?"

"We had some dancing in the homeschool network," she says with an embarrassed laugh. "It was...uh...modest."

"Oh really?" I say with a devilish smile, and I quickly step in to turn her around, holding her hips from behind. "Nothing like this, then?"

"No," she laughs, blushing furiously and turning her head toward me. "No, not at all. I like it, though," she adds in a lower tone, and I let out a rumble from my chest as I grind against her. The song changes to a slower beat, and I realize that we must be the only interesting people on the floor tonight, in the DJ's point of view.

I'm glad for that. Charity deserves the attention she's been deprived of too long. She deserves some appreciation.

I squeeze her hips and feel my cock pulsing against her ass as we move in a slower rhythm, and I lose myself in our shared heat.

"Hey," she finally says, turning around and putting her arms on my shoulders, folding them behind my neck and looking into my eyes as we dance closer. "This is all really new to me, but...thanks for getting me out here tonight. I think I like it."

I grin, and I feel a rare blush coming to my face.

"I think I like you, too," I say in a low, husky tone, and in the dim, colored lights of the club, we let ourselves get lost in each other's eyes. Nothing else matters in those moments that we sway together, and I can almost forget the dire situation that brought us together.

The song eventually ends, and we end our moment of enchantment to head to the bar and get another drink.

"Another mojito?" I offer, smiling at Charity as we lean up against the bar. She keeps a smile on her face, but when I look at her, I can tell something has changed.

Something's wrong.

She leans into me and whispers.

"We're being watched."

My blood runs cold, but I keep my own smiling face looking at her, keeping the same act that she has going.

"Where?"

"Back of the club. He's looking at his phone right now, you can look."

For the slightest of moments, I let my eyes leave her to scan the room, eyeing the shadows. When a familiar figure comes into sight, my heart skips a beat, and I slip her hand into mine, giving it a squeeze and leaning in to kiss her on the cheek.

But when I kiss her, I whisper my own message.

"We need to leave. Now."

She nods and giggles as if I just told a funny joke. She's getting remarkably good at this cover story. I leave a $100 on the bar and head for the exit, and she keeps up with me at a leisurely pace, not drawing any attention to us.

As soon as we're out of the bar, as I'm already formulating a plan for gathering our things and checking out of the hotel as soon as possible, I'm trying to hold myself together, because what I just saw could mean that the whole plan is unraveling around me.

The man at the back of the club wasn't some detective or officer.

It was Gabe.

And we weren't supposed to meet until much later.

Something is very wrong, and I have a bad feeling in my gut.

CHARITY

I wrap my arms around Jake's waist and lean into his warm back, resting my cheek against his shoulder blade. As usual, I can feel the powerful muscles tensing and flexing just under the thin fabric of his shirt, and it thrills me in a way I could never put into words.

He feels so strong, so capable, and it's comforting to know that he has such a tight grasp on the situation around us.

Or at least, he seems to.

He notices things that go over my head. He reads the room, feels out every vibration, good or bad, and is decisive enough to make quick, difficult choices without much struggle. It's almost as if he survives by pure instinct alone, always able to sense danger or trouble around the corner before it becomes a real problem. I can definitely understand how he's been able to get by doing what he does.

It's a nearly impossible life to lead. I don't have to be an expert in contract killing or criminal lifestyles in general to know that much. He's managed to fly under the radar, do ridiculous things, eliminate dangerous, important men, and yet still get by without getting caught. He seems to never lose his cool, even under extreme duress. When I'm out of my mind with panic, he's smooth and in control. When I'm overthinking everything and honing in on all the millions of ways it could go wrong, Jake is in the moment, dodging obstacles and rushing back into the safety of the shadows.

I know, logically, that being close to him makes me a target. It makes me an accomplice. I'm guilty by association, and I'm not too naive to realize that the kinds of people Jake has to interact with in this seedy underworld wouldn't hesitate to cut me down alongside him if I got in the way.

I don't have the experience or the strength to fight back and protect myself from nefarious forces lurking in the darkness. But Jake does. And even though I know it's probably crazy to trust him the way I do, I can't help it.

My heart tells me that he won't harm me. Not on purpose, not by accident. The way he holds me, the way he takes care of me, even the way he looks at me —all of that proves to me that with Jake, I am safe. No matter what. Maybe there was a time when I feared him more than anything else. At first, I saw only danger when I looked at him.

After all, he did rip me out of my quiet, unassuming little bubble and carry me into the flames. But when we are together and we trust one another, working like a team, those flames cannot burn us. We stand side by side, hand in hand in the fire, unburned and unscathed.

I don't have any idea what the future holds, but in my booze-addled mind, right now and right here on this motorcycle with Jake, I feel strangely good. Almost euphoric. Not even the unnerving presence of the other man can shake the feelings still rolling over me from our time in the club.

His body pressed against mine, his face bright and smiling, happy to be with me, spinning and clinging to one another in the eye of the storm. No one and no thing has ever made me feel this way before, and even if it ends in tragedy, I feel lucky to be on this ride with him right now. For better or for worse; that's what they say, isn't it?

I'm with Jake until the end or until he sets me back down in my dull corner of the world, for better or for worse. And I don't have to tell him this. He knows.

He reaches down to place his hand over both of mine where they're clasped together over his taut abdominal muscles. He gives my hands a pat and a squeeze, and I smile against the fabric of his shirt, nuzzling into his shoulder as the cool wind whips around us. This town is going to sleep, the lights flickering out down every block as the hours creep quietly toward midnight.

I know I should be frightened, but I'm not.

I'm only excited and a little sleepy.

Because when we get back to the hotel, I know what I want to do.

I plan to crawl into bed beside Jake, cuddle up to his broad chest, feel his strong arms close around me. The two of us, cocooned in the hotel bed sheets while the neon light of the sign flashing bright and dark through the wide window. I want to feel every inch of his body pressed up to mine. I am tingling all over just thinking about it.

Maybe we'll just fall asleep like that. I would be okay with sleeping. But perhaps there will be something more. Some new forbidden fruit to taste, some exciting mystery experience to unfold. Jake knows all the ways to make my body thrum and sing, and I have a feeling he has been holding back all this time.

He could do so much more to me, and while that might scare me if it was someone else, it's not like that with Jake. I trust him. He's proven to know what to do. I may be a novice to the ways of sex and love, but he seems to be an expert. I don't care where or how or with whom he learned it all, as long as he keeps showing me new ways to feel so, so good. I can hardly wait.

I press a gentle kiss into his shoulder and he tilts his head back to rest against my forehead for a moment. Everything feels so smooth and breezy, so simple. It's anything but simple, I know, but in this moment it's hard to believe we're caught up in a web of calculated risks and lies. My real life, the slow and empty existence I have carried out for twenty-one years, seems light-years away now. I'm a different woman now that Jake has plucked me out of the suburbs and dropped me into the thick of the battle.

I wonder what it will feel like when I go home. *If* I go home.

How will I ever fit back inside the narrow mold I left behind?

I'm interrupted from my thoughts by the sensation of Jake's cell phone vibrating in his pocket. The vibration travels up to my thigh, and at first it almost gets lost in the tremble of the motorcycle itself, the engine loud enough to drown it out almost entirely.

But Jake cautiously reaches into his pocket, pulls out the phone, and then I feel his body go rigid as he looks at the screen.

The motorcycle slows down and he gently pulls it to the side of the road, still sitting on the motorcycle but resting on one foot while he answers the call. I listen silently and nervously. It must be an important call for him to pull over during our getaway drive.

"Mom?" he answers softly. My heart does a somersault in my chest. I can just barely hear a panicked female voice on the other end of the line, but I can't make out what she's saying. Still, the fear in her tone is evident even without the script.

"Okay. Calm down. It's gonna be fine. I'm on my way. Hold tight," Jake assures her. "Yes, I'll be there as soon as I can. No, don't call the police. Keep the doors locked and the curtains drawn. I'm coming home. Love you, too."

He hangs up the phone, slips it into his pocket, and revs the engine back to life, pulling a hairpin turn and jetting off in the direction we came without a word of explanation. I open my mouth to ask what's going on, but then I remember that he probably won't be able to hear me over the roar of the engine. So I just hold on, close my eyes, and settle in for the drive.

The two of us are on pins and needles over the

hour and a half drive toward the outskirts of Philly where, presumably, his mother lives. All the while, we keep silent. Jake is fully ignoring the speed limit signs, but keeping to darkened back roads. My anxiety is mounting by the minute, and by the time we pull into a quiet neighborhood in Willow Grove, I feel like I might throw up from nerves. He slows down once we're in a residential area, and I can feel every muscle in his body tensing up as he looks around, eyeing every yard and alley with suspicion.

Now that the engine is quieter, I lean in and whisper against the shell of his ear, "Jake, what's going on? Why are we here?"

He's silent for a long moment, clearly trying to scan the area closely. I feel bad for distracting him, but I'm on the verge of major panic here. I don't know the severity of our situation or what to expect. I'm still exhausted, though by now my buzz has worn off. Now I'm just anxious to figure out what's happening.

Finally, Jake replies softly, "My mother is in trouble. Or thinks she is."

I gasp and nuzzle closer to him, clinging for support. "Uh oh," I mumble.

"Uh oh is right," he says grimly.

We make a few more turns, going deeper into the neighborhood until we reach a dead end street with rows of bungalow houses, small and modest. I wonder what secrets lie behind each of these humble facades, what kinds of fears lurk in the neatly-trimmed hedges.

This is not a rich neighborhood—that much is obvious. But it looks homely and comforting, the kind of place where one could eke out a pleasant, quiet living and keep to oneself.

I have a feeling that's the kind of life Jake would live if given the chance, and that realization kind of breaks my heart. We're opposites in that way. I've been craving excitement, adventure, anything to break up the monotony of my real life. Jake has been thrust into a life of danger and uncertainty, but all he wants is stability. Suddenly, I feel kind of guilty for ever resenting my easy, sheltered life.

The motorcycle putters up a driveway at the end of the street, right by the dead end sign. It's a slouchy, low-slung navy blue house with canary-yellow trim and a stark-white front door. The rose bushes out front look to be perfectly maintained, and I have to smile to myself in spite of my nervousness.

This home looks warm and inviting, even if it's nothing impressive, even though the windows are all dark, as if no one's home. The motorcycle stops and Jake hastily helps me down, leading me by the hand to the front door.

He doesn't even have to knock before the door inches open to reveal a sliver of a sweet, middle-aged female face looking very anxious. She has the same bright green eyes as Jake, though her dark hair is streaked with silvery threads. Her face lights up when she sees who's at the door, and she hurriedly beckons us inside without a single word.

Jake pushes me into the house, nods to his mother, and then sneaks back out, leaving me alone with her. His mother quickly locks the door again, and reaches for my hand as though it's the most natural thing in the world. She holds a finger to her lips to keep me quiet, and leads me down the darkened hallway to a tiny but cozy sitting room. She urges me to sit down on the old-looking floral loveseat and I oblige. Finally, she speaks.

In a soft, cautious voice she says, "Would you like some tea?"

I give her a smile and, though my impulse is to decline, I get the sense that she wants to keep her hands busy. So I nod. "Oh, yes please."

"What flavor do you like, dear?" she asks, in a near-whisper.

I shrug and smile pleasantly. "Any kind is fine by me. Thank you."

She nods and putters into the adjoining kitchen, where a kettle is already starting to wail. I lean around and watch as she pours two cups of tea with trembling hands. I bite my lip, wanting to go help her but knowing that if she's anything like her son, she won't accept my assistance. She carries the tea back on a silver tray, the porcelain tea cups vibrating and clinking as she sets it on a small coffee table between the loveseat and armchair.

"Lavender earl grey," she whispers.

"Sounds lovely. Thanks," I reply, taking my cup.

"What is your name, dear?" she asks, still so softly.

"Charity," I answer. "What's yours?"

"Maude," she says. "Charity is a pretty name."

"So is Maude," I reply, smiling.

"Sorry to call you both out here in the middle of the night, but I thought perhaps I saw someone prowling around outside and, well, I got frightened," she explains sadly.

"Don't apologize. Jake would sooner pull his own arm off than put you in danger," I tell her honestly. She chuckles, her face brightening.

"I know. He's such a good boy. Always takes care of me, even though he doesn't have to. It's strange, you know. I used to think I had to protect him from the world, but nowadays, he's the one protecting me. And he always has, even before I fell ill," Maude explains.

She warms to the topic, clearly chuffed to have a chance to talk about her beloved son. "You know, my ex-husband, Jake's stepfather, was a terrible man. Jake saw that even before I did. He's forever been good at reading people. If he likes you, it must mean you're a good person."

I blush, staring down into my cup of tea. Luckily, she continues. "I'm so happy he's found someone. After he rescued me from his stepfather, he kind of closed himself off. He never brought another girl home. I think he was too afraid to let himself be happy. My Jake—he's such a sweetheart. So attentive. He just poured all his energy into taking care of me. He still does. I've tried to tell him to live his own life, let me handle my problems. If I fail, it's my fault, not his. But he refuses to let go. He works so hard, Charity. So hard," she trails off, getting misty-eyed.

"He adores you. He'd do anything for you," I tell her. She nods.

"Yes. He's almost too good. If not for him, well, I wouldn't be here now, I'm afraid. I just worry that he's so caught up trying to save me that he's going to forget to save himself," Maude laments, shaking her head.

I open my mouth to answer, but then I hear the jangling of what sounds like a dog collar, and the pitter-patter of paws on tile. Moments later, a medium-sized white dog with brown patches and blue eyes comes trotting into the room, tongue lolling. When he catches sight of me, his tail starts wagging uncontrollably and he rushes over to jump up onto the loveseat beside me, laying his head in my lap. I giggle and almost spill my tea, I'm so delighted and surprised.

"Samson, calm down," Maude says, laughing gently. "Oh, I don't know why I bother. He can't hear me. That dog is deaf as a brick wall."

"I didn't know Jake had a dog," I whisper, scratching Samson behind the ears.

"Mhm. Samson's been with us, oh, about five years now. He's the only remaining puppy of the litter our old dog, Goldie, gave birth to. The others all got adopted out, but Samson was the runt. And being deaf and all, we just knew he was safer here with us. Poor Goldie. She was such a good girl, but boy, did she have a hard life. My ex-husband—he didn't treat animals any better than he treated humans. But Goldie was so sweet. She never fought back, not even once. Samson's just like her. Well, except for being deaf and a lot dumber. We love him, though. Especially Jake. That dog is his life," Maude explains, grinning.

There's a faint scraping noise from across the house and both of us freeze up, but then Jake comes walking into the sitting room, and we realize he must have come in through the back screen door. He grins when he sees Samson in my lap, but the dog nearly trips over himself in his haste to get up and greet Jake.

"Good boy, Sammy. Oh, I missed you, too," he gushes, kneeling down to hug his dog, whose tail is wagging so hard it looks like it might detach and go flying at any second.

Jake looks over at his mother and smiles. "It was just some bratty neighborhood kids skulking around. I scared 'em off," he says, and we both sigh in relief.

"Oh, good. I'm sorry for dragging you out here for no reason," Maude sighs.

Jake walks over and kisses her on the forehead. "No worries. I'd rather be safe than sorry. But I do think we should stay the night here, just in case. That okay with you?"

Maude beams happily, wrapping her shawl more tightly around herself. "Oh, yes! Of course. I'll make us breakfast in the morning! I'm sure you're both exhausted. There are fresh linens in the closet, and you could sleep in your old room in the basement." She yawns.

Jake pats her on the shoulder. "Go ahead to sleep, Mom. I'll make up the bed and stuff. It's way past your bedtime."

She giggles and nods as she hoists herself up and trudges away. "You're right about that. Oh, it's been lovely to meet you, Charity. See you both in the morning."

"Same to you. Good night," I reply brightly. As Maude disappears down the hall, Samson the dog follows after her like a white shadow. Jake gestures for me to come with him. He puts an arm around me and leads me down another hall and downstairs to a basement, which looks less creepy and more cozy than one might expect. It's a simple, comfortable bedroom with framed pictures on the walls, and even though there are no windows, there are string lights around the headboard of the bed, casting the room in a soft glow. I wait patiently while Jake retrieves some sheets and makes up the bed, and I can't help but watch his muscles flexing as he does so. Even though I'm exhausted, there's a part of me that doesn't want to sleep. I want to stay awake, lying next to Jake and feeling his body so close to mine.

"It's been a long day," he whispers. "Come here."

I saunter over to him and he folds me in his arms, hugging me close as he sways from side to side. Finally, I can exhale the breath I didn't know I was holding. No matter how strange and scary things get, I always feel safe in his embrace.

Still, seeing Jake's mother has reminded me of my

own parents, worried sick and frustrated with me for what they will view as 'rebelling.' I murmur, "I have no idea how angry my parents will be when I go home. I miss them, but I'm dreading it."

"I can understand that," he says gently, stroking my hair.

"It's odd, you know. I always dreamed about breaking free, but I never expected it to be like this," I muse aloud. "I never thought being with a... a *man* could feel this way."

"There's so much more I could show you," he whispers, sending a thrill down my spine.

I lean back and look up into his handsome face, those green eyes shining with promise. I bite my lip and muster up the courage to ask quietly, "Will you?"

He contemplates it for only a moment before leaning in to kiss me deeply.

The taste of her lips pressed against mine awakens my body to a feeling it's learning to love very quickly. I hold her face in my hands as we touch, and I push her against the wall, running my hands down her shoulders to her sides, resting on her hips. I squeeze her, feeling her push against my crotch and her needful moan spill into my mouth as our tongues touch.

She has always been very careful, very conservative when it comes to matters of what happens in the bedroom, but this time, I feel something different in her. Her hands do some exploring of her own. She keeps her hands on my shoulders, but soon, they start to explore downward to my pecs. She traces their outline with her thumbs, then lets her fingers slide further down to my abs, right where they rest while she's on the back of my motorcycle.

I've often felt her there, squeezing me and being held in my hand, but I've never felt her get so bold in how she touches me.

"Have you been waiting for this, Charity?" I growl in a low tone as our kiss breaks, and I put my hand over hers, running it around my abs and letting her feel just how hard I am. "Feel it. Enjoy all of it. Everything you want."

She leans her head back against the wall, exposing her neck to me, and I move my face in to kiss it. I'm gentle at first, but I soon feel my more primal desires getting the better of me, and I open my mouth to let my teeth graze her neck. I bite some of it gently, teasing her with the sharp edges of my teeth and never pinching her too hard, but letting her know that I have power over her here. Meanwhile, her hands trail further down.

She touches the V pointing toward my crotch, feeling how even my hips are impeccably sculpted. I have kept myself in peak physical condition ever since I could start developing real muscles, and I never want to let them lose their shape. Not as long as I have something to fight for, and Charity is reminding me that I'll never run out of that.

"You know what my body does," I say in a low,

husky tone. "You know how well I use it to kill. You've seen it firsthand."

I look her in the eyes, and she stares back at me with innocent wonder and fascination. I have her utterly entranced in me, in everything that I am and represent. And the longer I gaze at her, the more I realize that she has me under the exact same spell, even though I never noticed it creeping over my mind. It's intoxicating. *She* is intoxicating. And I've never known more clearly than then that I want to utterly lose myself in the aura of another human being.

"Do you still fear me?" I ask. She seems surprised at the question. I take her chin between my thumb and forefinger, then run the tip of my thumb over her lower lip, feeling how soft and wet she is, still eager for more of me.

"I do," she says.

"Do you want to leave?" I ask.

"I..." she hesitates, but she seems to be searching for the words for what she wants to say. "I don't know, to tell you the truth. I thought I knew the answers to everything about this whole...*thing* we have going on, but I don't."

I give her a soft smile through my rugged face.

"I'm glad we have that in common," I say.

I kiss her again, and this time, she wraps her arms

around my torso as I walk us back to the bed and sit down with her. We explore each other's bodies, feeling our warmth and energy in a messy spell of passion before I start to guide us down to the sheets. We kick our shoes off as we get further up the bed, feeling our way inch by inch until we're side by side like lovers, facing each other in the dim light of the basement and feeling our hearts swell.

"I want to see you," I say, reaching over and cradling her cheek in my hand. "All of you."

She nods softly, nervous, and I lean over to kiss her on the lips before I help her work her top off. It has barely hit the floor before her bra is unhooked, and I pull that off her as well, slowly, as if opening a precious gift. She's nervous, and she watches my face carefully as I look on her topless.

My cock swells so greatly that my pants feel tight, and I feel a desperate need for release building up inside me that I won't be able to ignore for long.

I reach forward and grasp her breasts in my hands, squeezing them gently yet firmly in my large, rough hands, and I push her onto her back, pinning her under me. I kiss her, toying with her breasts with my fingers, mapping out every detail of her chest. I could spend hours here just tracing my fingers over her body, feeling how soft and supple her flesh is, how warm and delightful it is to hold. I want to possess her and give her everything I can all at the same time.

I break the kiss to work my way down her and slip off her pants, working them and her panties off with the help of her wiggling hips and squirming legs. In a matter of seconds, Charity is naked before me, and I'm still fully clothed.

"Is..." she starts, then pauses, biting her lip. I raise an eyebrow at her. "Is it weird that I kind of like this? Being naked while you still have all your clothes on?"

I give a deep chuckle, and I loom over her, narrowing my eyes. "Why do you suppose you feel that way, hm?"

"I...it makes me feel like you're..."

"Your captor?" I finish for her in a deep, husky growl, and as soon as the words leave my mouth, we meet each other in a fierce kiss. My hands are possessive and dominating on her, guiding her into every position I want as we make out and grind against each other on the bed. Her moans get more frequent and deeper as her bare skin brushes against my rough, air-dried clothes that I've worn on me as I hopped from city to city, sometimes state to state, always on the run.

Charity has been anchored to the home for her whole life, and I've been away from it. We couldn't be more different. And that difference makes the moment all the more thrilling as our bodies meet.

But I won't deny her my body forever. Soon, I stand up on my knees, straddling her, and I pull my shirt up and over my head. I look down at her as she stares at my torso, admiring me as if I'm a statue, almost as hard as one. Her eyes go to the thick bulge outlined in my pants, and I slowly unbutton the front of my jeans to reveal it inch by inch, like a slow strip tease.

Finally, I let my cock free, and it sticks straight out, swollen and ready for Charity.

The girl's mouth falls open as she sees it, and for a few moments, she's speechless, even though she clearly wants to say something.

"Touch it," I say in a low tone. She obeys, reaching up and wrapping her hand around the base of my shaft carefully. She's so delicate that it's almost funny. She runs her hand up and down it with the lightest touch I've ever felt, and I feel a smile growing on my lips. "You can grip it more firmly, it won't hurt me."

"Are you sure?"

"I've lived with it for twenty-seven years," I say. "I'm sure."

She tightens her grip a little to the point that I feel all the heat of her palm and all its softness spreading warmth through me like comforting fire. I let my head fall back slowly as I groan, and that seems to encourage her as she touches the tip of my cock, feeling it twitch at the touch of her thumb.

This girl is everything I could ever want. I thought that when I first saw her, and now I know that instinct is right. Something about the way she touches me feels so natural and comfortable that you'd think we've known each other for years.

I can't contain myself any longer. I gently pull away from her, then move down her body and push her legs open, bringing my face down to her. She gasps as I breathe in the heady scent again, and I see that she's already slick and ready for me.

"Wait!" she says in a sharp whisper. I freeze, looking up at her with a questioning gaze. She winces, almost apologetic for having interrupted me, but she opens her trembling mouth to speak. "I want to taste you, too."

My eyebrows go up, and my cock twitches at the thought of that small mouth and full lips wrapping around my cock. It's a thought that makes my heart beat faster, and I know I can't deny her anything she wants.

"Do you, now?" I growl.

She nods, blushing furiously. "I mean, I don't

want you to stop, but...I want both. Can we do both?"

I can't help but laugh, and I reach up to kiss her on the mouth, stroking her hair. "Of course we can. Follow my lead."

I gently move her to the side of the bed, and I crawl to the other side, laying down on my side in the opposite direction. She watches me carefully, and when she realizes what position I'm moving toward, she speaks up.

"Oh, this is sixty-nine, right?"

I have to fight to hold back a laugh, but I'm not laughing at her naivety. There's a kind of simple innocence to everything she says that makes me feel at ease, and I've never felt like that around a woman I'm in bed with. It's refreshing, and I'm getting more fond of it by the minute.

"Something like that," I say. "The idea's the same, but we're going to take it a little easy. This is your first time doing something like this. Like I said, follow my lead."

I move toward her, curling myself in just enough that she can reach my cock, and at the same time, I push one of her legs up and put my face between her thighs, feeling myself get basked in her warmth. Once again, her pussy is up against my face, but before I can let my tongue out to greet it, I feel something warm and hot on my cock.

I thought I would have to guide Charity into being bold enough to take my cock into her mouth, but she isn't shy once it's up in her face. I feel my whole crown get enveloped by full lips, and she immediately presses her tongue to my bulging crown. I let out a groan, and she pushes her hips into my face, clearly pleased with herself.

While her tongue enjoys itself around the tip of my cock, I let my tongue out to massage her pussy, and I hear her gasp mirror my own. As a circle, the two of us feel one another with our mouths, sending warm embers of delight through our bodies together.

I start slowly, but not as slowly as I was when I gave her her first time. My tongue finds its way to her clit immediately, and rather than torturing her with a painfully slow buildup, I let my tongue flick out and brush against her clit from the very beginning. Her hips squirm at the familiar feeling, and I start letting my tongue out in steady, rhythmic motions, swirling it in little circles with each stroke before withdrawing and swallowing more of her honey.

The way her tongue explores my cock is clumsy, but it has a fresh curiosity to it that my manhood can't get enough of. I'm stiffer than I have been in a long time as she takes more of me into her mouth, and she moans into my shaft as I feel her warm lips massage me. Her hot, wet mouth takes two more inches of my cock into it, and I feel like I'm being bathed in luxury. Her tongue runs up and down the top of my cock while the soft underside gets pressed up against the roof of her mouth. It's all soft yet firm at the same time, and I'm so slick that I could be inside her pussy.

I let my tongue get bolder and cover more ground, delving deep into her pussy and lingering there, swirling it around and massaging every part of her that I can get the tip of my tongue on. I expand my tongue wider and let it rub against more of her with each stroke, and the slow but steady flow of honey gets even sweeter in my mouth.

She takes half of my whole girth into her mouth, clearly seeing this as a challenge by now. One of her hands plays with my balls while she lavishes my cock with attention, and I feel myself pulse and throb in her mouth as a reward. She gasps as I finish exploring the depths of her pussy and start flicking my tongue against her clit again, and I feel her starting to well up with tension just as a drop of my precum beads up and drops into her mouth.

I hear a sweet, beautiful gasp from her as she tastes me, but that soon melts into an even more loving groan as she takes as much of my cock into her mouth as she can fit. My crown touches the back of her throat, and her throat tenses as if she's about to gag, but she pulls back before that can happen, and I feel the tip of my cock against her soft palate.

My tongue gets faster and faster on her pussy, and I feel her mouth moving in a barely conscious rhythm with my strokes. I get firmer, harder, faster by the second, and we soon have a perfect rhythm with one another. She's far better than I'd expect from someone with no experience, but I'm prouder of her each time we touch.

Finally, I feel her hips squirming, and I hold them in place as I lick her at a steady pace into an orgasm. She lets out a deep, long moan as she comes, and I massage her pussy all the way through it, just like last time, while her tongue never stops lavishing my cock with attention.

When it's over, I gently pull my cock away from her, and she gets the message and releases it. She looks down at me with an almost disappointed face, hungry for my cock. I turn around on the bed and kiss her. Making her taste her own honey never gets old.

"Why did we stop?" she asks, nearly panting.

"I want to finish inside you," I growl, reaching for

my pants. But when I get my wallet out, I clench my jaw. "Damnit! No condom."

"I don't care," she says quickly, looking up at me desperately. "I need you inside me, Jake. I need you *now*."

I look at her with a hard glare, feeling my cock so tight and ready for release that it's almost painful.

"Are you sure?" I ask. "I won't hold back anything."

She looks at me with eyes so full of desire and lust that even I'm surprised, and her full, swollen lips open to utter a single word.

"Good."

CHARITY

My heart is pounding so hard and I can hardly remember to breathe.

I feel both scorching hot and shivering cold at the same time, every cell in my body on high alert as I sit perched on the bed, gazing up into Jake's gorgeous, leaf-green eyes.

I feel like I could stay here forever, just watching his handsome face, noting each and every tiny, almost imperceptible shift in mood and tone crossing those rugged features. Sometimes, when I look at him, this sensation of overpowering desire and affection seizes hold of me, and it's so new and unexplainable that it kind of scares me a little bit.

I have never known feelings like this.

The closest I have ever come to it was when I developed a crush on a professor of mine at college.

When I went to an all-girls' college, I never expected to run into the kinds of typical "boy-crazy" feelings my parents warned me about.

And truth be told, they didn't expect it either. I'm sure they assumed all of my teachers would be crusty old men with paunchy bellies and balding, shiny heads. But one of them was a young man with dark hair and a ready smile. He looked like one of the guys in a magazine I would read sneakily on the bus ride to and from campus, and I was entranced.

Still, the feelings I had for my professor pale in comparison to the raging, swirling maelstrom of powerful emotions I feel for Jake. It's like the two of us have been swept up into a tornado together, spinning above the earth, surrounded by danger and dread, but miraculously safe when we're together. The first night we spent together, I was still so afraid of him, I was too scared and paranoid to sleep.

Now, I don't want to sleep because I don't want to miss a single moment with Jake. I have no idea how long we're going to stay together. After all, we were never meant to end up stuck with one another in the first place. Jake is a loner, that much I can tell even before finding out more about him. He doesn't love easily. He doesn't bend. And in his world of risks and traps, there is little room for a wild card like me. I know I'm a liability to him, to his way of life, to his mission to protect and save his mother.

Yet, he hasn't let me go. I am still here. And I plan to stay as long as he'll have me, whatever happens. I have a feeling this can't last forever, but I'm willing to settle for just tonight, as long as we make the absolute most of it. By the way he's looking at me, those eyes smoldering, his body tensed and ready, his cock stiff and straining for me—I can tell that he plans to make tonight as amazing as possible, give me some sweet, sexy memories to take home with me when I go.

I want to freeze-frame his image in my mind, crystallize this powerful moment in memory so that I can reflect on it in my future lonely nights. Because I know that once I leave him, or rather he leaves me, I won't recover from this. Not that the fear and danger itself will scar me—I don't care about that. But it's the beautiful things I won't forget. It's the way he touches me, reverently and dominantly at the same time. It's the way he kisses me, the way the three syllables of my ordinary name sound extraordinary on his lips.

It's the little things that will haunt me forever, but before we part, I need one big event to capture and hold close like a firefly in a mason jar. To light my way through the dark once Jake is gone and out of my life. I will never forget him, so why not make tonight a night to remember?

I can see clearly that Jake is thinking the same thing. The answer is plain on his face as he reaches for me, his hands sliding down my shoulders, down my arms, to grasp both of my hands.

He raises them up and kisses both palms delicately, sending a shiver down my spine, and then he reaches around to cradle me backwards on the bed, laying my head on the pillow as he straddles me. I stare up at him, biting my lip, blushing, nearly trembling with anticipation and worry.

I don't know what it will feel like, having his cock inside me.

I've read so many stories in my magazines, and it seems to be different for everyone. Some say it feels good, some say it hurts so badly they can't help but cry. Either way, I'm prepared to accept whichever answer it is. As long as Jake is the one touching me, it will be good. That's all I know.

"You truly are so beautiful," he murmurs, looming over me and licking his lips. Suddenly, I feel so small, so fragile underneath him. Jake could destroy me, shatter me into tiny pieces if he so chooses, but he won't. He wouldn't. He wants me to feel good, and I have no doubt that he knows just how to make that happen.

He strokes my cheek with two fingers, following the shape of my cheekbone down to my jaw, to tip my chin up as he leans down to brush his lips against mine. It's soft at first, tantalizing, like he's teasing me. And then a little harder, his lips parting and his tongue probing into my mouth. A tingle rolls down through my body and I moan into his mouth, arching my back and trying to press up into him.

I'm getting impatient now, wanting him to fill me up and make me feel whole again. Growing impatient, I reach down between us to lightly stroke his massive, glorious cock, and it gives me a little thrill to feel him shudder at my touch. But then, to my dismay, he grabs my wrists and pins them up over my head before dipping down to kiss me again. He breaks away and gives me a gentle but mischievous smile.

"Patience, Charity," he whispers.

"I don't want to wait any longer," I reply breathily, pouting. "I just want you to take me."

I can tell by the flicker of dark lust in his eyes that he wants the same thing, but he's trying his hardest to hold back. Despite all his warnings, I fear nothing. I know what I want, and for once, I'm not afraid to ask for it.

"I know you don't want to hurt me, but you

won't. I promise. Whatever you can give me, I swear I can handle it, Jake. Please," I murmur softly.

He contemplates my words for a moment, looking totally conflicted, and then he smirks.

"Okay," he growls. "As you wish."

And with that, he takes his cock in his hand and leans back slightly, guiding the engorged head of his shaft to my slick, aching opening. I brace myself up on my elbow, holding my breath and watching wide-eyed as he circles my hole with his cock, teasing and easing me into the sensation. I'm entranced by the movement, which sends little tingles of pleasure up through me. My pussy is on fire, tight and clenching, pulsing with need.

The tension in my body is almost painful, and I'm desperate for a release. Jake is equally tight-wound and I know he needs this as badly as I do. He looks up and locks eyes with me, asking a silent question.

Are you ready?

I give him a nervous nod, and he starts to push inside of me. I let out a little yelp of shock and pain and collapse back onto the bed, breathing hard and fast as his cock threatens to split me in two. He's so big, and my cunny is so tight. It feels as though I could shatter for real, just burst into little glass shards and never be put together again.

And yet, it feels good, too. Satisfying in a way

that defies explanation. The pain radiates across my pelvis as he spears into me slowly, until the tip of his cock is pressing against my thin barrier, the threshold that has kept me a virgin all this time. Jake is gritting his teeth, his hands curled into fists gripping the sheets on either side of me as he steadily, cautiously presses on, not wanting to break me, but needing to push past my hymen.

"Oh my—oh my gosh," I gasp, closing my eyes tightly and arching up to meet him as he shoves through that aching boundary, straight through to fill me up, stuffing me to the hilt. A burst of mind-numbing pain mingled with incredible pleasure over-whelms me and I cry out, whimpering and shaking as the head of his cock strikes against a deliciously pleasurable spot deep inside me. It's almost too much to bear, and yet I don't want him to stop.

"More," I choke out. "More."

Jake pulls back out, and I open my eyes, looking up at him in desperation and worry, but then he just pushes back inside of me, faster and harder this time. Again, he strikes against that special spot and I shud-der. A ragged moan rolls out of my throat as he pulls back and pushes in again and again, building pres-sure and moving faster each time.

He's getting less cautious, treating me less like a fragile piece of china and more like, well, a woman. I roll my hips, clenching involuntarily as he fucks me harder and faster. He leans down to kiss me, swallowing down cry after cry from my lips. The rhythm is pounding now, his cock sliding in and out of me with effortless, natural ease. We fit together so well, his huge cock nearly fully sheathed inside my virginal pussy.

"It feels so good," I mumble, reaching up to dig my nails into his muscular back as he pumps into me hard. He's starting to lose control now, with less regard for my pain. That's exactly what I want. I need him to use my body, fill me up, pump me full of his cock until I can hardly breathe. Before long, I'm convulsing with one powerful climax after another, his shaft spearing into what my magazines call a g-spot, pummeling my insides until I'm an incoherent, gasping mess beneath him.

"Fuck, you're so tight. So perfect," he snarls, his hips snapping back as he pistons in and out of my cunny. I arch my back and groan, wrapping my legs around his waist. He reaches down under me to hold me up as he fucks me harder and harder, gaining momentum. His rhythm is growing erratic as he starts to use my body for his own pleasure, beads of sweat appearing at his temples. His beautiful face is twisted in an expression of gorgeous ecstasy, his cock pounding my pussy with abandon.

There's not a force in the universe that could stop us now. We're moving together as one moaning, writhing tangle of limbs, desire mounting us higher and higher, closer to the ultimate peak. Finally, with a few more rapid thrusts, Jake and I come at the same time, both of us going rigid and grasping at one another as we cry out each other's names.

We stay this way for a long few moments, just reveling in our shared bliss and clinging to each other for dear life. And then he cradles me back down and kisses me on the lips, my cheeks, my forehead, the tip of my nose, making me giggle. Still inside of me, Jake cups my face in his hands, peering into my eyes with wonder and fondness.

It's like the two of us are wrapped up in a big, warm, joyous cocoon, clutching each other, neither of us wanting to move and disturb the sense of peace and safety over us. But finally, he slides his cock out of me, and we sit up, our backs against the headboard. I lean my cheek on his shoulder and he kisses the top of my head. I look down to see my honey glistening along with his seed and a slight tinge of pinkish blood leaking out of my pussy. There is a throbbing undercurrent of pain, but it's faint underneath the reverberating waves of warmth and pleasure I'm still reeling from.

"Was it everything you wanted?" Jake whispers softly.

I nod and smile, tears of happiness burning in my eyes. "It was everything. And more."

"Good," he answers, kissing me on the top of my head and pulling me into a hug.

"I can't believe I waited this long to feel this way," I murmur. "But I'm glad I did. I'm glad I waited for you to come along. I wouldn't have wanted anyone else."

"Come on. Let's get cleaned up. There's an en suite right there," Jake says, smiling. He takes me by the hand and helps me gingerly slide off the bed. I wince a little, having to take a rather wide stance as I walk at first. The pain is definitely there, but it doesn't bother me somehow. It feels like a small price to pay for the pleasure and joy I received in exchange.

The two of us step into the tiny shower stall, rinsing off our bodies even though we don't take the time to wash our hair. Jake lathers up my body, lovingly cleansing every inch of me, kissing me throughout the whole process. I have never felt so adored, so taken care of. When we're done, he gives me a towel from under the sink. We dry off and I yawn as we pad back over to the bed. I'm so exhausted and overwhelmed with the events of the past few days. All I want is to crawl under the sheets and snuggle up to Jake and fall asleep for as long as fate will let me.

But just as Jake and I are putting on some of his old t-shirts and boxers to sleep in, there's a blood-curdling scream from upstairs. We both freeze up, looking at each other wide-eyed for a moment. Then Jake bolts for the stairs, and I follow after him, my heart racing. He bounds upstairs and throws the door open, racing into the living room with me two steps behind. I nearly slam right into Jake as he comes to an abrupt stop, raising his arms up. I peer around him and gasp, clapping a hand over my mouth at the horrific sight before us.

There's a man holding Maude with an arm around her chest and the other arm grasping a large knife, the sharp point of which is aimed straight at her throat. It doesn't take long for my instincts to determine who the man is.

I don't know how I know, but I know. It's the man from the hotel room. The one who hired Jake to carry out the executions. And he looks maniacally angry.

There are certain things that set people off in ways they can barely control, ways that tap into very basic fears and trigger equally base responses. I've never been able to stomach threats against my mom. That reaction was beaten into me as a kid by my stepfather, and I've never lived it down. It's the whole reason I'm in the situation I'm in now.

And just like those dark days when I was too young and too small to defend either myself or her, I find myself unarmed but burning with fury.

Anger burns white-hot in my blood as I look at the sight of Gabe holding my mother at knifepoint. It feels like the whole world is falling apart around me, and I feel a deep, cutting coldness in my heart. This is my worst nightmare. This is the one thing that I feared most when I first fled my home at sixteen and turned to crime—that it would come back to bite the one person I had left to care about. Now, I have two that I care for, and they're both in danger because of my actions.

I can't live with that.

But since I'm unarmed and he has a knife on her, he has taken away the one means I have of fighting back against that.

"Gabe," I growl in a deep tone, slowly holding up a hand and glaring at him with a deadly serious gaze. "You are making a *very* big mistake. Let her go and set the knife down. That's your one warning."

"Are you fucking serious?" he laughs, a cruel grin on his face and an unstable spark in his wild eyes. "After everything you put me through, you think you can give me orders when all the cards are in my hand? I don't think so."

"I don't know what you're talking about, Gabe," I said in slow, careful words, not making any sudden movements. One of my arms has gone up to half-wrap around Charity protectively. "The job is done. You know that. We had a deal."

He scoffs, shaking his head. "You have no idea what you're up against, do you?" he muses. "Of course you don't."

"Then help me understand," I urge him, desperately wishing he would lower the knife just long enough for me to lunge at him and snap his feeble neck in my bare hands.

"Here's something you can understand," he says. "You're going to meet me at the bridge east of town at dawn. Call the cops, and not only will she die, but I'll take you down with me for the deal we had together. If I get so much as a fucking *shadow* of an idea that you're following me, she'll be dead before you even get close enough to see my face. I lowjacked your bike, and if you take it off, it'll deactivate. If I see your signal so much as flicker, you won't even see her body. Do I make myself perfectly fucking clear, *Jacob*?"

I want to tear this man's head off. He's thorough, I'll give him that, but every fucking thing about him fills me with fury that I have to keep bridled just a little while longer.

"I said, 'do I make myself clear?'" he bellows again, and my mother winces, clenching her eyes shut as she tries to fight back the stream of tears trailing down her face. There are no words for the pain the sight gives me. I heard those same words from my stepfather too many times to behave like a rational person around a man like Gabe.

He doesn't deserve that dignity any more than my mother deserves this kind of treatment.

"Yeah," I say, nodding slowly. It takes every

ounce of strength I have to keep my cool. "I hear you, Gabe. You're in control. I'll comply." I have to talk to him like a child throwing a tantrum, because that's all he is. There's no room for bravado here, not until he gets that knife away from my mother.

"That's right," he snaps in a lower tone, and he turns his face to my mother. "Alright, bitch, we're going for a ride. Walk with me slowly, backward." While I hug Charity tighter to me, we both watch in painful anticipation as Gabe slowly backs out to the front door with my mother in his arms, ordering her to open the door and let them out. "You two don't move until you can't see my headlights anymore," he snarls.

And just like that, he's gone.

Every nerve in my body wants to race after him, to pull him out of that car and beat him to a bloody pulp...but I can't risk my mother's life. That would be more than a risk. It would be a death sentence. As soon as the car engine starts up, I watch the lights start to move outside, and Gabe's car pulls away, rumbling down the road.

"Jake..." Charity's voice says softly, but I've already let go of her. I put a hand on the wall and lean against it, my head down and my body nearly shaking. I clench a fist so tight that my fingernails cut into my palm. I want to throw my fist into the wall, but I won't do that. I did that enough when I was younger to learn what an unhealthy and damaging habit that is.

Besides, I've got to save that rage for Gabe.

Charity sets a small hand on my shoulder, and I feel a bit of the tension in my back relax at her touch. I never thought she could have a calming effect on me in the middle of a situation like this, but she does, and I'm grateful for it. So grateful that I open my palm and lay my hand over hers, squeezing her gently. When I turn to face her, my eyes are rimmed with red on my stony, rugged face, and I can see her heart breaking as she looks up at me.

"She's going to be okay, Jake," she assures me, trying her best to be comforting and soothing. "We're going to get her back."

"Charity...this is even worse than it looks," I say in a low, raspy tone. Once the headlights are out of sight, I stride toward the window and peer out it, staring with a hollow gaze. "That man, Gabe. He's the one who hired me to handle this contract. He was the man in the room with me when I first found you. You probably guessed that already."

She nods softly.

"I've walked into a trap," I say. "She's in danger because of me."

"You can't think of things that way," she insists,

stepping forward and hugging me from behind. I lay a hand over hers on my stomach, and I close my eyes.

"I must. I won't shy away from my mistakes."

"He sounded like you two have bad blood," she says.

"That was as much of a surprise to me as to you," I say. "I wouldn't knowingly take work from a rival. If I've wronged him in the past, I didn't know it. I should have seen it coming. I've made enemies. Of course I would have pissed someone off along the way who noticed. I started so young that I wasn't as careful as I am now."

"You can't blame yourself for this, Jake, you know that. You can't hold yourself accountable for every single mistake."

Oh, but I can.

"Charity," I say, turning to face her, looking at those gleaming eyes, "there's more to it than that. The way I started this life is so closely tied to this house that I can't escape it."

"What do you mean?" she asks. I take a deep breath.

"I...did not start this life of killing when my mother was diagnosed with cancer. It started well before then. I've told you about how life was for me in the early years, growing up with my stepfather. He got physical with both me and her. Often."

Charity's eyes are wide and shimmering, and her mouth falls open as she realizes where this is going. I don't draw it out.

"One afternoon, it got out of hand. Far worse than it should have. My mother dared talk back to him for hitting me when I forgot some groceries on the way home from school. He was already drunk." I've never told this story before, and as I relive it, I feel old feelings creeping through my nerves like poisoned thorns digging into me. I have to stay strong.

"He laid into her, hard. He wouldn't stop. I wake up sometimes with the sounds in my ears, ringing. We were in the garage. He was waiting for me when I rode in on my old bicycle. At the time, he...he had been building something in there. I barely remember what it was. A shelf, maybe. There was a long cast-iron rod leaning against the wall. I didn't think. I just swung it."

Charity's hands go to her mouth, but I'm staring out the window again.

"It caught him in the side of the head, and he went down immediately. My mom was passed out, either from getting hit too hard by him or from the shock of what she saw. So, I put her on the couch with an ice pack and cleaned up, made it look like an accident. I've been on the run ever since. I knew I couldn't stay home. I sent my mother letters, but it was never safe for me to come back until much later."

"Jake…" Charity pauses, and a long moment of silence passes between us. "I don't blame you."

I chuckle. Maybe she really has come around to my way of thinking.

"Thank you," I say. "But it doesn't matter now. Only one thing does right now," I say, turning to look down at her with purpose. "Getting her back safely."

FOUR HOURS LATER, dawn is just starting to breach the darkness of night as my bike approaches the bridge. My headlight shines down its foggy length, and Charity's grip around my waist tightens when it reveals the form of Gabe standing there, my mother in front of him, in his grasp.

"No sudden movements," I tell Charity in a low tone as I stop the bike, leaving the headlight on to light the way as I climb off the bike with her slowly. "We still don't know what he wants. It's probably me. That's the best case scenario," I add. "Follow my lead."

"I'm with you," Charity whispers.

I'm wearing my jacket again, and this time, I'm armed. Gabe surely knows that. The element of surprise is completely absent. He has me at a disadvantage in every way, down to the fact that he knows how I usually operate. Bastard played me like a fiddle, and I don't even know why.

"Nice ride?" Gabe calls across the bridge as I start to make my way toward him slowly. "Hey hey hey, hands where I can see them."

I hold my hands palms-up at my sides as I approach, slowing down.

"What is all this for, Gabe?" I call. "Why all this trouble? Why hire me? Why not settle things back at the house?"

"Because I wanted to give you a show," he growls. I'm close enough now that we can talk in even tones. Barely ten feet separates us, but as I start to step closer, he presses the knife to my mother's throat.

Mom's eyes are looking at me in terror, and I can see the silent plea in them. She hasn't spoken yet, but I can tell she's trying as hard as I am to keep calm. To say this is a delicate situation is an understatement.

"Level with me, Gabe," I say, my anger barely contained. "I can't help you if you don't tell me why you're doing this."

"Help me?" he spits with a cruel laugh. "You could have helped me by dropping dead eleven years ago before you ruined my life!"

Eleven years?

"I…" I start. "There was no way I could have known you back then, Gabe."

"No, you didn't," he says. "But we had another link. I had a family, Jake. It wasn't perfect, but it was mine. I had a loving mom and dad just like you. Dad wasn't around that much, but that didn't matter. It worked. We made it work. We adapted. We survived."

There's a crazed edge to his voice, and in the headlight filtering past me, I can see the madness and obsession in his eyes as he goes on.

"But one day, Dad didn't come home. Just vanished. Mom was heartbroken. I didn't know what to do. I had to come back from school to take care of her. But I wasn't about to just let that sleeping dog lie. No. I did some digging and found out what happened to him."

My mind is already racing, and I realize that eleven years ago, I was just sixteen.

The year of my first kill.

My eyes go wide.

"Turns out, Dad had a whole 'nother family," he growls, and I can hear the pain in his voice. "A wife and a kid. He told Mother and I that he went on long business trips. I suspected Mother was naive, and that he was having an affair, but it went deeper than that. He was *married*. He even used a different name. You have no idea how hard it was to track him down. You can't imagine how it felt when I learned that he wasn't even alive."

Charity gasps as it clicks for her, too, and my jaw sets. Gabe glares at me with raw hatred, hands almost shaking.

"He died under suspicious circumstances with his fake family. Blow to the head. The police couldn't even get enough evidence to pin it on this bitch," he adds, jerking my mother and holding the knife closer to her throat. "I cased her house, you know. Watched her. I could tell it wasn't her. But her son was missing. Police suspected him, but couldn't find him. That's how I found you," he says with a murderous edge to his voice. "When I finally tracked you down and contacted you, I know exactly who the fuck you were. Step-sibling," he chuckles darkly.

"Gabe," I say slowly, sincerely. "If you had any idea...*any* idea what kind of man your father was, you wouldn't be fighting for him right now."

"Shut up!" he shouts, and my mother shudders in his grasp, trembling. "I didn't come here to bargain with you. I came here to let you watch me cut your mother down the way you cut down my dad."

"Maude is innocent, Gabe!" Charity shouts, stepping forward and surprising both me and Gabe. "She's had nothing to do with any of this. She's just as much of a victim as you!"

Gabe stares at Charity, mouth gaping as he struggles to find words. He seems to falter, and in that moment...my mother acts.

In the split second that Gabe is distracted, Mom twists away from him, scrambling to the ground and trying to crawl away. Gabe shouts as she breaks loose, and he raises his knife to bring it down on her while she's on the ground.

I'm faster.

It took about a second to clear the space between us, and I catch Gabe around the hips in a tackle just in time for him to plunge the knife into my shoulder. He hits the asphalt hard, and I don't even feel the knife. I knock his hands out of the way and punch him across the jaw so hard that I hear teeth scatter across the pavement. Reaching over my shoulder, I grip the handle of the knife still buried in my muscle, and I yank it out.

I raise the knife, still dripping with my own blood, ready to plunge it down into Gabe's face.

"Jake!"

It's Charity's voice.

I freeze.

In the headlight behind me, I can see Gabe in my shadow. His face is sheet-white, and his hands are back. I have him completely in my power, trembling in pain as blood pools in his mouth and he waits for death. He's a miserable rat I helped create, even if it was his own twisted mind that pushed him this far. A drop of blood falls from the knife onto his forehead.

Charity knows all that just as much as I do.

And if I want her...I have to be better than him. I have to be above my base instincts.

I don't lower the knife. I turn it, pointing it at him in a more level, controlled manner, locking eyes with this monster for a few painfully tense moments.

"Charity," I say in a low tone. "Call the police. Tell them there's been an attempted murder and kidnapping. I have him restrained."

CHARITY

"Sir, I understand that you want to go in and see your mother, but I do have just a few more questions I need to ask you first," insists one of the police officers who was called to the scene.

We are all at the hospital now, after having followed the ambulance here on Jake's motorcycle. When Jake called the police on Gabe, rather than killing him, the cops were adamant about taking Maude to the hospital to make sure she was unharmed and that the stress of the situation hasn't caused any complications with her illness.

Jake was resistant to the idea, wanting to just take her home and look after her himself, but I gently agreed with the police and urged him to let them take her. At my encouragement, he finally gave in and allowed the ambulance to take his mother to the hospital, but only on the condition that we be allowed to tag along and for the cops to go to the hospital for our interviews.

Of course, the cops are frustrated, too, by the fact that the doctors took some time to patch up Jake's shoulder before turning us loose to the police again. By now, they're all pretty exasperated and impatient.

"There's no way in hell she's going to that hospital without me, so if you want to interrogate me, you'll have to do it there," Jake had insisted. His stubbornness flustered the cops, but it kind of makes me smile, to be honest. He loves his mother and will gladly piss off the police to stay by her side. That kind of commitment and loyalty is something I find utterly beautiful about him. There are few people in this world Jake cares about so deeply, but once you're in that tight-knit circle, he will bend over backwards to help you.

"You already have the perpetrator in custody," Jake says to the cop flatly. "Why don't you just ask him these questions? I need to see my mother."

"They're just trying to help," I remind him gently. I look at the cop and fix him with a stern expression, one I must have picked up from my own mother over time. It works, to my surprise, and the cop swallows hard, looking intimidated. I could almost giggle at his reaction, but I manage to maintain my composure.

I straighten up and force a polite smile instead. "Any chance I could help fill in the gaps in our testimony so that Jake here can see his mom? I was there, too, and I have no problem answering questions on his behalf."

The cop looks back and forth between us, unconvinced at first. I can tell he has a sense about Jake, like he can just feel the aggression and danger simmering just under the surface. I get it. Between the two of us, Jake is definitely the more interesting figure in the eyes of the law. A tall, muscular, powerful-looking man is more likely to set off alarm bells than a petite, polite young woman like me.

"Come on, man. She's really sick and she's got to be traumatized by this whole situation. Why can't I just go see her? She needs to see a familiar face. My mother gets nervous in the hospital. Too many bad memories over the years, you know?" Jake explains, his voice softening as he speaks from the heart. The police officer seems to soften, as well, finally hearing the humanity in Jake's pleas. The genuine concern. He heaves a sigh and nods, waving his hand to dismiss Jake from the interrogation.

"Alright, alright. You wore me down. Go see your mother," the rookie cop relents. Then he seems to remember that he's supposed to seem tough, and he stiffens up, puffing out his chest and narrowing his eyes at Jake. He wags a finger warningly and adds, "But I'll have more questions for you later, okay?"

"Got it. Fully understood," Jake replies over his shoulder, already heading down the hall in a hurry to his mother's hospital room. He gives me a quick, subtle smile, too.

I nod in response, silently assuring him that I won't give away any incriminating information. I'm on Jake's side, no matter what.

He may be a killer, but he's a good man, and if there's anyone who deserves to get a second chance, it's him.

His methods are cold, but his intentions are warm. I know that. I understand it. Jake lives within a shade of gray, and his actions reflect that. Desperate times call for desperate measures, and I can't hold it against him that he's willing to sacrifice the lives of terrible, evil men, and risk his own life in the process, to save his beloved mother.

It's more than just understanding, though; I admire him for it. Few men in this world would go so far to protect the ones they love, but Jake? He doesn't even hesitate. He sees the best option and jumps for it without a second thought.

I turn back to the cop with a bright, cheery smile,

ready to lie through my teeth to protect the one *I* love, even if it means putting myself at risk.

"So, what do you want to know?" I ask helpfully. A flicker of a smile crosses his face, and I can tell he's already bought and sold and wrapped around my finger. There is a definite upside to being small and innocent-looking. Men don't fear me. They trust me. They believe me, thinking I'm too naive and too sweet to lie.

That's a mistake on their part, but I am certainly going to use it to my advantage. I weave a lush, detailed story about how Gabe has been stalking and threatening Jake and his mother, about how he's been trying to blackmail and extort Jake into carrying out darker and darker deeds. But that Jake has been strong and steadfast, trying to take the noble path and keep right.

The cop scribbles down my tale frantically, trying to keep up. I even manage to summon up some Oscar-worthy tears to add flavor to my story. Before long, the rookie officer is eating out of my hand, wide-eyed and slack-jawed as he listens to my testimony, almost forgetting to write it down, he's so enraptured.

When I'm done, he says, "Uh. Thank you, ma'am. That was... a lot of detail. You know, you're a good storyteller. And you have a good memory."

I smile and shrug through my sort-of-fake-tears. "Thanks. Do you have everything you need? I'd really like to join Jake and see what the doctors have to say about his mother's condition, if that's okay," I suggest.

He nods. "Sure. Go ahead. Thanks again for your time."

I smile and swivel around, walking away with my heart racing. I can't believe I just lied to the cops. But I know that for Jake, I would do it again. And again.

HOURS LATER, the doctors finally released Maude from the hospital. Not wanting to put her on the motorcycle in her fragile condition, we hire a car to take us home. I ride along with Maude while Jake drives the bike along behind us.

When we get back to his mother's house, we ease her into her bedroom, helping her into bed. She looks pale and exhausted, but her eyes are bright and shining with relief. Jake takes some time to cook her a bowl of soup and a sandwich, along with some sleepy time tea to help calm her addled nerves. While he cooks, I sit next to her in bed, the two of us chatting and watching a soap opera.

Once Jake comes in with the food tray, he kisses

her on the forehead and leaves her to it, urging her to eat before taking a nap. She hardly slept at all last night, and in her condition, it's important that she keep up her strength and give her body time to recover from the trauma.

So we close the bedroom door and go back downstairs to the basement where we won't interrupt her nap. I walk over and collapse onto the bed with a heavy sigh, my whole body feeling like an anchor is dragging me down. I'm so tired, and yet wide awake at the same time. Just having Jake in the room is enough to set my nerves on fire. But he only sits on the edge of the bed, looking wan and overwhelmed with worry. I scoot over to perch next to him, concerned.

"What's wrong? The doctors said she's physically unharmed. Gabe didn't hurt her," I remind him. Jake looks at me with those beautiful green eyes and I can see unfathomable sorrow.

"It's the money I'm worried about. Even just the ambulance ride and her hospital stay today will put us in the red," he explains softly. "And if Gabe was just setting me up, then that means there will be no more payoff from the work he hired me to do. I was counting on that just to get us through, Charity. Now we have nothing. How am I going to pay for her treatments? What if I have to take her off the transplant list? She needs bone marrow, but we can't afford it."

I bite my lip, feeling my heart break. And here I thought we were finally out of the woods. "Bone marrow?" I repeat quietly. "Jake, does she have cancer?"

He nods. "Yes. For years now. It would come and go, into remission and back into danger again. But this time it's bad. Really bad. And it's so expensive. I don't know what to do."

I've never seen him so vulnerable before, and yet so strong and resolved. I know he would walk on glass to the ends of the earth to help his mother, but it's looking hopeless. Then, a bizarre idea comes to me and I'm not sure if it's worth mentioning, but Jake looks so downtrodden I feel like I have to.

I mumble, "Well, my father—he's an oncologist. I never think much about it because he doesn't talk about work when he's at home with my family. But I've overheard him mention something about a clinical trial before to my mom. Sometimes they talk about serious stuff when they think nobody is listening."

Jake looks at me with an expression of mingled confusion and interest. I go on. "What if—hear me out—I try to get your mom in on that trial?" I suggest.

Those green eyes widen. "You would ask that? Do you think he would go for it?" Jake asks, the slightest twinge of hope in his voice.

I shrug, smiling softly. "I could try!"

"After all I've put you through, you would do that for someone like me?" he inquires, his dark brows furrowed. He looks utterly bewildered by such kindness. I get the sense he hasn't seen a lot of unprovoked kindness in his life. Perhaps that's why he's so dead set on saving his mother. She's one of the few bright spots in his whole universe.

"You never meant to involve me in all this, Jake. I know that. I was in the wrong place at the wrong time. And you could've killed me. You could've abandoned me in the woods. There were so many points... I know it was a huge risk to take me along with you. I was a liability. I still am, probably. But you took care of me. You've shown me things—beautiful things—I never would've seen otherwise. You're a good man in a terrible predicament. I get that. And besides, you stopped yourself from killing Gabe. You could have. He deserved it every bit as much as those other evil men you eliminated. But you didn't. You took the high road. That shows me something important. That shows me you're reformed. You can be... good," I conclude.

"You believe in me," he says, and it's so full of

awe that it's almost a question. I giggle and lean into him.

"Yes. I do. But you have to promise me that your old life, the dangerous one, is over. You have to be better. For your mother's sake, for my sake, but most of all, for your own sake. Promise me that, and I'm yours. Forever," I tell him.

He grins mischievously and replies, "Now look who's throwing out an ultimatum."

I laugh. "Yep. My turn now. So, what'll it be, Jake?"

He leans in and kisses me passionately, then breaks away to murmur, "As if there was any question. I will do whatever it takes to keep you, Charity. I never thought I could feel this way about anyone. Ever. I thought I was doomed to a life alone in the shadows. But you've proved to me that there's so much more. That even a man like me could find peace. Even a man like me could have an amazing, beautiful, pure-hearted girl like you. And this probably goes without saying, Charity, but I love you. I do."

My whole body tingles and I can't help but grin, throwing my arms around him as he reaches to pull off my shirt. He kisses me as I climb on top to straddle him, rolling my hips against the growing bulge between his legs.

"I love you, too. More than anything. I never want to be apart from you, Jake. Come what may, you're mine and I'm yours," I promise him fervently.

"Good. Because I'm going to claim you either way," he replies, his voice turning husky with need. I want it hard and fast this time, the adrenaline ramping up despite how tired we are. Just being near him is like a jolt of energy straight to my soul.

He slips off my clothes and his, then positions the head of his cock at my glistening hole. I'm already slick and eager for him as he pushes inside, both of us moaning and clutching one another. Even though I'm on top, I follow his lead. He grabs my hips and starts to move me back and forth, up and down, riding his cock. His large hands slide up to cup my breasts, rolling my sensitive, perky nipples between his fingertips as I writhe and whimper on top of him.

Jake leans in to kiss my ticklish neck, sucking delicate purple bruises under my skin, his hips thrusting up to match my rhythm. We move together faster and harder, losing ourselves to the crashing waves of lust and need. We want to be as close as possible, unified in every moan, every movement. He grabs my ass, kissing me on the lips as we mount closer and closer to orgasm. His cock is spearing into my g-spot repeatedly, giving me goosebumps and making me cry out in desperation.

"I love you, I love you," he whispers against the shell of my ear, the two of us rocking together in tandem.

"I'm so close," I gasp, my fingernails digging into his strong back.

"Give it to me, Charity. I want to feel you come all over my cock," he hisses. The ticklish, delicious sensation of his warm breath on my neck is enough to push me over the edge and I whimper through my climax.

Jake slams up into my pussy, coming only seconds after me. As I feel his hot seed explode inside my twitching cunny, he cradles me close. Jake rests his forehead against mine while we come down from the high, both of us so caught up in the moment and full of love. I don't know what the future holds, but I know I won't go it alone. Not anymore. I have no fear, not with Jake by my side. Together, we can do anything.

"Oh my god, five of them!"

The sound of my mother's endless gushing paired with Charity hovering around us taking a dozen pictures a minute keeps the goofy smile plastered on my face as I help deliver yet another big, healthy puppy from the newly non-pregnant dog's belly, I'm sitting cross-legged in the living room of my mother's house, and Sampson—the proud father of the litter—hovers around anxiously, panting, but trusting me to handle the mother of his new puppies.

"Sampson," I chuckle, picking up the last of the bunch and beckoning my dog to my side, petting him as he sniffs his newborn. "Look at him! He looks just like his papa, doesn't he?" Sampson's tongue lolls out to the side as he smiles up at me, and I feel my heart swelling to the point of bursting as Charity kneels down beside the rest of the pups with tears in her eyes.

Charity's parents sit on the couch across from us while the three of us dote over the pups, and even they can't keep their usual stodgy faces. The whole room is full of smiles and loving comments as we photograph the puppies to no end.

This has been what life has been like the past few months—at long last, nothing but smiles.

Gabe went to prison for multiple accounts of murder, kidnapping, and attempted murder, thanks to our efforts. The evidence against him was over-whelming, and I was able to clear myself of all connections to him before the investigation started in earnest. The police are looking for a mysterious hitman, or several hitman, but they'll never find me. I've made sure of that. I have to put that life behind me, and I'm glad to see it go.

The life I have now is more than I could have ever dreamed of.

As Charity kneels beside me and giggles delight-edly with two puppies in her arms, peppering them with kisses, the engagement ring on her hand glim-mers in the afternoon sun filtering through the window. It's the very same one I bought her when we were pretending to be engaged. I told her that I threw the ring away with the clothes, but in truth, I kept it in my pocket all the while. I couldn't bring myself to get rid of such a thing that made her so happy.

I presented it to her right after she found out she was pregnant with our baby.

She's just now starting to show, thankfully, and she looks more beautiful with each passing day. The bump in her belly can grow without any more worries, because as it turns out, Gabe did indeed have the other five-hundred thousand in cash at his hideout—one of the other things I beat the police to.

With a million dollars, safely in savings building interest —except for what I take out to take care of my mother's treatment—there's a bright and beautiful future ahead of all of us. With a body like mine and as much a love of bikes as I have, it will be easy to find work as a mechanic, but that safety net will never leave us in the meantime. I can work as much or as little as I like, and it only further pads the life we're going to build together.

And on the subject of my mother's treatment, I unexpectedly have Charity's father to thank for the sudden turn for the better things have taken. Me proposing to Charity and demonstrating to them that I'm a good, reliable man was essential to getting on her parents' good side. In turn, we set up my mother with the care of her oncologist father.

My mother's cancer is in remission, and I've had no trouble getting her the treatment she needs. It's never the end of the road with this kind of thing, but thanks to our intervention, my mother is going to be able to have the long, happy life she deserves.

"I...think we might have room for a puppy in our house, if you're interested in selling any of them," Charity's mother speaks up with a reluctant smile, and I grin at her from across the room.

"I think that can be arranged," I say. "Don't want to feel empty nest symptom with one of the siblings out of the house now, do you?"

"It'll be good for them," her father agrees with a chuckle. But the way the two of them are looking at each other, I get the sense that they'd like something else to help bring them together, as well. Meanwhile, Charity beams at me, but she looks away the second I glance back at her, blushing.

"Okay, but just so you know," Charity says, "if you do, you *have* to bring the puppy to our wedding. And Aubrey's, because yes, you're coming to that one too—it's my last chance to be a maid of honor right before my wedding."

Her father opens his mouth to protest, but her

mother lays a hand on his knee and gives him a stern look. He smiles, rolls his eyes, and nods.

"I think we can arrange for all of them to be there," my mother says, looking up from the feeding pups and smiling. "Maybe by then one of them will be big enough to be a little ring bearer."

"Oh my gosh, *please!*" Charity gushes, looking at me with stars in her eyes.

"You're looking at me as if I wouldn't be as excited as you about that?" I chuckle, and I lean over to kiss Charity on the cheek.

This is our life now. This is the light that we've given birth to out of the blackest darkness.

And from here on out, that's all it's going to be.

Brighter and brighter every day.

THANK you so much for reading! I hope you enjoyed <3 If you have a moment, please leave a review. Other readers are dying to know what you thought.

I have plenty more bad boy romance for you, so make sure you check out my other books on the next couple of pages, and sign up for my newsletter to be notified when I have a new release on the way!

~Alexis Abbott

The Assassin's Heart

Killing For Her

Abducted

Stepbrothers:

Ruthless

Criminal

Standalones:

Betting on Love

Hunter's Baby

I Hired A Hitman

Vegas Boss

Rock Hard Bodyguard

Innocence For Sale: Jane

Redeeming Viktor

Romance:

Falling for her Boss (Novella)

Most Wanted: Lilly (Novella)

Bound as the World Burns (SFF)

Erotic Thriller:

The Dangerous Men Series:

The Narrow Path

Strayed from the Path

Path to Ruin

ABOUT THE AUTHOR

Alexis Abbott is a Wall Street Journal & USA Today bestselling author who writes about bad boys protecting their girls! Pick up her books today if you can't resist a bad boy who is a good man, and find yourself transported with super steamy sex, gritty suspense, and lots of romance.

She lives in beautiful St. John's, NL, Canada with her amazing husband.

facebook.com / abbottauthor

twitter.com / abbottauthor

instagram.com / alexisabbottauthor

bookbub.com / authors / alexis-abbott

pinterest.com / badboyromance

youtube.com / AlexisAbbott

ACKNOWLEDGMENTS

Thank you to my amazing Patrons. I'm constantly humbled and grateful for your support.

Ramona Cabrera
Melissa Hedrick
Virginia Swanson
Dawn Daughenbaugh
Don Doss
Stacie Currie

If you'd like to join them — and get my ebooks or paperbacks — you can find me here on Patreon.
https://www.patreon.com/alexisabbott

www.ingramcontent.com/pod-product-compliance
Lightning Source LLC
Chambersburg PA
CBHW061619190726
48288CB00007B/2394